I0743397
1
catgirl doctor
Brandon Varnell
Illustrations By Liremi

catgirl doctor

Volume 1

By Brandon Varnell

Art by Liremi

Catgirl Doctor, Vol. 1
Copyright © 2020 Brandon Varnell & Kitsune Incorporated
Illustration Copyright © 2020 Liremi Art
All rights reserved.

To see Brandon Varnell's other works, or to ask for permission to use his works, visit him at www.varnell-brandon.com, facebook at www.facebook.com/AmericanKitsune, twitter at www.twitter.com/BrandonbVarnell, Patreon at https://www.patreon.com/BrandonVarnell, and instagram at www.instagram.com/brandonbvarnell.

If you'd like to know when I'm releasing a new book, you can sign up for my mailing list at https://www.varnell-brandon.com/mailing-list.

ISBN: 978-1-951904-05-0

dedication

This page is made in dedication to my amazing patrons.
Without them, my characters would never get lewded by so
many wonderful artists:

Aaron Harris
Alarinnise
C.L. Holgrahm
Chace Corso
Dominic Q Roddan
Edward Lamar Stephenson
Emery Moore
Feitochan
Forrest Hansen
Jacob Flores
Jacob Wonjo
James Leon-Moore
Kevin
Kevin Aulinger
Lane Watkins
Lucid Fayt
Matthew Wallace
Max A Kramer
Michael Moneymaker
Peter Barton
Rafael Eriksen
Seismic Wolf
Syed Hamdani
ToraLinkley
Travis Cox
William Crew

table of contents

chapter 1   1

chapter 2   21

chapter 3   39

chapter 4   61

chapter 5   85

chapter 6   109

chapter 7   139

chapter 8   159

chapter 9   189

chapter 1

Chris Redford sat in the very center of the lecture hall, dutifully jotting down notes as the teacher standing on the lecture podium continued talking.

"Catgirls are anatomically quite similar to humans. Their bodies have all of the organs that we humans do, but this does not mean they are identical to humans in every way, shape, and form."

Surrounding Chris were several other students; a man on his left was leaning back in his seat, arms crossed with a look of disinterest on his face. On his other side was a young woman with curly blonde hair. Unlike the lazy bum on his left, the woman was typing notes into a laptop. There were actually over thirty students aside from himself in this room. That just went to show him how many people were interested in becoming a Catgirl Doctor.

"While their ears and tails are the most obvious physical differences between catgirls and humans, their reproductive system is also quite a bit different."

The teacher standing on the podium was a young woman with dark hair, dark eyes, and pale skin. If her eyes had been red, Chris would have suspected she was a vampire. She was also quite short and very flat. He'd heard a rumor once that his teacher had been mistaken for a child by one of the students. This rumor also mentioned that the student in question was admitted to the hospital.

As she lectured them, the teacher manipulated a small remote in her hands. A large screen situated against the wall behind her suddenly lit up. What appeared on the screen was a diagram detailing the anatomy of what, at first glance, someone might mistake for a human female. It was only after noticing the triangle-shaped ears and the tail behind them that anyone unfamiliar with this class would realize otherwise.

The diagram suddenly split into two. The figure on the left was that of a human, distinguishable because it had no cat ears or tail. On the right, the figure had cat ears and a tail.

"As you can see from these two diagrams, catgirls have the same reproductive organs as any human and the way it works is very similar to a normal human's reproductive system. There's the vulva, the mons pubis, the labia, the clitoris, the urethra, and so on. You should have studied sexual reproduction already in your standard sexual education courses, so we're not going into that. What I'm going to discuss right now are the differences between catgirls and humans."

The teacher manipulated the remote again, which caused the human diagram to be replaced with the diagram of a cat. Chris paused in his note taking to check and make sure all of his facts were straight. He placed his hand on the paper, feeling the smooth material graze his fingers, and used his index finger to trail underneath his notes. Each point the teacher made had a bulletin point next to it. Anecdotes were written underneath certain parts of the teacher's lecture. He was sure they were correct.

"The biggest difference between humans and catgirls is that catgirls periodically go into heat after reaching puberty, just like cats," the teacher stated. "Puberty for a catgirl starts after they reach sixteen years of age. Just like regular cats, their periods of being in heat are influenced by seasonal changes in the amount of daylight that's available. A catgirl's usual cycle is between January and September, and a catgirl will also keep going back into heat every fourteen to twenty-one days until she has bred with a male or the amount of daylight decreases in October."

"So basically, what you're is saying is that all catgirls are THOTs who want a man's dick," said the man on Chris's left. He looked like a very typical delinquent. His hair was slicked back, though he did have a pair of bangs framing his narrow eyes. He wore a rumpled jacket and pants that became even more disorderly as he leaned further back in his chair.

His words caused mixed reactions among the students. A few men and women snorted and tried to contain their laughter, but several, like the blonde woman on Chris's left, glared in disgust at the man. Chris did his best to ignore him.

"Prick," the blonde woman mumbled.

"What was that?!" the man said.

The delinquent turned his head to glare at the blonde, but the woman on Chris's right didn't back down, and he soon found himself trapped between two glaring individuals. It was enough to make him wonder why he'd chosen this seat in the first place. Oh. That's right. These two had decided to sit in their respective seats after him.

He almost sighed.

"Mr. Jason Barker, do you want to remain in my class?" asked the teacher, her eyes locked onto the delinquent. "Because if you do, I suggest you keep your mouth shut. I've heard about you from the other professors. You might have been able to get away with being a douche canoe in their class, but if you are not respectful in mine, I will kick your ass out of here faster than you can say 'doctor.'"

The crass words spoken by the teacher caused a few students to erupt into silent applause. Jason, on the other hand, gnashed his teeth together as he stared at the teacher, who met his gaze with an even look. Chris thought he saw sparks clash between the two of them. That was definitely his overactive imagination, however.

"Tch. Whatever."

Jason looked away. The teacher waited for a moment, perhaps to see if he would act out again, and then continued her lecture.

"There are several ways to deal with a catgirl who has gone into heat. As far back as even fifteen years ago, the Catgirl Protection Bureau created a career for young men who would act as breeders. Their job is literally to satisfy a catgirl until her heat ends. However, with the advancement of medical technology, we've now managed to produce a medicine that has the effect of calming down a catgirl while she's in heat. She might still act a little affectionate toward her catpanion or her guardian, but she won't try to outright mate with any male in sight." The teacher paused for a moment. "Unfortunately, not only is the medicine expensive, but it contains highly addictive substances. For this reason, use of the medicine is tightly controlled and can only be administered by a certified Catgirl Doctor. There have actually been several reports of people stealing this medicine and using it to enslave catgirls by making them addicted to the substance. It is also because the medicine is so tightly controlled that breeders still exist."

"Hmph. Maybe I should have become a breeder," Jason said. "That sounds like a much better profession than being a stupid doctor."

"A scummy man like you would never be accepted as a breeder." The blonde on my right snorted and wrinkled her nose as if she smelled something disgusting. "Breeders undergo numerous psychological and physical evaluations to make sure they are fit both mentally and physically to be a breeder. There's no way they would allow a trashy man like you to ever breed with a catgirl."

"What was that?! You want to say that again, bitch?!"

Jason stood up in his chair and turned toward Chris and the blonde, who looked like she was just as ready to throw down as he was. Chris wondered if he should just step away and let these two duke it out. However, before he could really contemplate his own course of action, the teacher stepped in.

"Jason Barker, I want you to leave. You are officially dismissed from my class. I'll be sure to file a report to the dean stating the reason you've been kicked out."

A shocked look crossed Jason's face, but it only lasted for a moment before he gritted his teeth together. With anger blazing in his eyes, he stomped down the stairs, glared hatefully at the teacher, and then stormed out of the room. The door slammed shut behind him and a tense silence filled the atmosphere.

"Now that Mr. Barker is gone, let's continue the lesson," the teacher said.

The lecture continued, and Chris did his best to ignore what had just happened, but he did wonder about that Jason character. Why would a man like that even bother taking a course on catgirls? He didn't seem all that interested in becoming a catgirl doctor. With that crass attitude of his, Chris wasn't sure the man even qualified.

"Unbelievable," the blonde woman muttered. "I can't believe a man like that was able to attend these courses. What was the board of directors thinking when they allowed him to attend our college?"

"I'm not sure." Chris shrugged. "But anyone who wants to is allowed to attend college so long as they pay the tuition fees and pass the entrance exams."

"That is true," the woman sighed. "Oh. I'm sorry. You sort of got caught between us, didn't you?"

"It's fine. I wasn't bothered by it," Chris said.

"You're a pretty unflappable person, aren't you?" The woman leaned over on her hand and looked at Chris with brilliant green eyes. "Even though two people were literally arguing right beside you, you didn't even bat an eye."

"If the situation really got out of hand, I would have stepped in," Chris said.

"Is that so?" The woman eyed him for a while longer, looking him up and down, before smiling. "I'm Anastasia, by the way."

"Chris Redford," Chris greeted her. "It's a pleasure to meet you."

The class didn't last much longer, and as the bell rang to signify the class had come to an end, everyone stood up and began packing their supplies. Chris closed up his binder filled with notes and placed it inside of his back. On the other hand, Anastasia closed her laptop, placed it inside of a case, and placed that in her bag.

Chris wondered if he should consider investing in a laptop. He didn't have much money because he was living off student loans and could only pay for apartment, college tuition, and food, but maybe he could take on a few commissions to earn some extra cash and invest in one? It would be nice if he could have all of his notes in a single storage unit instead of spread through multiple notebooks.

"Hey, Chris," Anastasia suddenly said. "Do you want to grab a bite to eat with me after classes?"

After slinging his bag over his shoulder, Chris paused and looked at Anastasia. Now that she was standing up, he could see that she was a well-endowed woman with a large bust and wide hips. Her waist was thin and looked toned from exercise. She had that perfect hourglass figure a lot of swimsuit models had. Combine that with her locks of scintillating blonde hair and green eyes, and Chris was certain most men would consider her their perfect wet dream.

He smiled and shook his head. "I'm sorry, but would you mind if I take a rain check? There's something I want to speak with Professor Shinomiya about, and then I'm heading over to my gym."

"Gym?" Anastasia blinked before looking Chris up and down. "That explains why you are so fit. All right. I'll let you take a rain check, but I expect you to cash in on it soon, you hear?"

"Sure thing," Chris said.

Anastasia left soon after. Chris watched as she walked out the door, waving goodbye when she sent him a wave, but then he walked down the stairs and toward the podium, where the teacher was sighing as if she had something on her mind.

"Professor Shinomiya?" he asked.

Airi Shinomiya was her full name. She was half-Asian. Chris didn't know much about her, not even what her exact nationality was (he thought she was half-Japanese because Shinomiya sounded like a very Japanese name), but she was the youngest professor in the entire college campus. She was only 26, making her just seven years older than Chris.

Professor Shinomiya had a preference for a clothing style known as Gothic Lolita. While her current outfit was a very subdued black dress, it had a variety of frills and lace. The front was buttoned up all the way to her neck. Her long skirt traveled a little past her knees, ended in a large gathering of frills, and hid the upper part of her black boots, which actually gave her an extra two inches in height.

"Mr. Redford." Professor Shinomiya straightened. "I'm guessing you have more questions for me?"

"I do." Chris nodded. "You mentioned that only a certified Catgirl Doctor can administer the medicine that can help ease a catgirl when she's in heat. Are there no occasions, like an emergency situation, where someone who isn't a Catgirl Doctor can administer them?"

Professor Shinomiya paused and considered his question. Chris patiently waited.

"There are a few situations where it is possible," she said at last. "There have been known cases where a catgirl going into heat can become dangerous to the catgirl in question. For example, catgirls can get zoonotic diseases that can become deadly if a catgirl goes into heat. During situations like this, it isn't always feasible to travel to a certified Catgirl Hospital every time she goes into her mating period, so we allow someone who has undergone the same evaluation tests as breeders to administer the medicine in our place. This is generally taken as a case by case assessment. If, after examining the catgirl, it is determined that her life is in jeopardy, we will have the catgirl's guardian take an on-site evaluation. Does that answer your question?"

"It does. Thank you very much."

Professor Shinomiya smiled at Chris. "You're a very diligent student. Out of the entire class, you are the only one who asks me these questions."

Chris wouldn't say he was embarrassed by the praise, but he did feel a little awkward. He only asked these questions because he was serious about becoming a Catgirl Doctor. Rubbing the back of his head, he tried to smile at his teacher, even though it felt a little stiff to him.

"That's just because I really want to become a Catgirl Doctor," he said, as if that was his only reason.

***

Sweat flew off Chris's face as he faced off against his trainer. The man before him was absolutely ripped, with powerful muscles, broad shoulders, and a chest and abs that looked like they were made of solid rock. His skin was incredibly dark, almost obsidian. He also had a buzz cut and a scar that went down his right cheek. While he looked intimidating, the friendly smile on his face was enough to put most people at ease.

"Come on! Don't let up!" the man barked.

"Hn!"

Chris darted toward the much larger man and threw two powerful but swift jabs, first with the left, then the right hand. Both jabs were blocked. The solid thud of his fists meeting his trainer's gloves echoed out from the point of impact. However, Chris didn't stop with just his punches and quickly launched a swift roundhouse at his trainer's legs. That was blocked when the man raised his foot. The attack thudded off his shin.

"Good! Excellent! Now let's see your defense!"

With his foot still raised, Chris's trainer lunged forward. His right fist flew in a powerful straight punch that looked like it packed enough power to pulverize a person's head. That was what it looked like to Chris, at least.

He avoided the punch by ducking low and backing off, but his trainer continued moving forward with quick shuffles, throwing several more super powered punches at him. Some of those punches were toward the face, but a few were aimed at his torso. Chris could swear he actually heard the wind howling when the punches passed by. He narrowed his eyes as he used the back of his hands to guard the attacks.

They continued trading attack and defense for several minutes. However, Chris eventually ran out of steam. When he grew sluggish, his trainer backed off and let Chris fall onto his hands and knees. His breathing had grown heavy, a sharp pain stabbed at his chest, and his shoulders heaved as he tried to suck in air.

"You've improved a lot," the man said.

"T-thank you… Captain…"

The man Chris called "Captain" was Tanner McKellips, a man who had served in the military for over twenty years. He was currently listed on the reserves. This kickboxing center was something he opened up as a means of killing time and helping others reach their fitness goals while learning self-defense.

Chris didn't think he'd ever need to know how to fight, but the fitness benefits were nice, and learning self-defense on the off chance that something *did* happen was a good bonus.

"I think we're done for the day," Tanner said. "Hit the showers and head on home. You coming in tomorrow?"

"I should be able to." Standing up, Chris rubbed some of the bruises on his body, which he'd gotten due to his own carelessness during their spar. He would have said Tanner didn't know how to hold back, but he'd also seen the man hit a punching bag so hard the sand burst out. "I have some commissions I need to work on, but it shouldn't be a problem."

"Good. Then I'll see you tomorrow."

With their lesson over, Tanner hopped out of the kickboxing ring and went over to where two young women were taking turns on the punching bag. As he began speaking with them, Chris looked around. Several other people were also hitting and kicking the punching bags. There were also a number of people using the sparring mats, which were located to his left and by the backdoor.

The scent of sweat reached his nose. Of course, it wasn't the people in the gym but his own sweat he was smelling. He wrinkled his nose a little as he grabbed his towel and hopped off the kickboxing ring. Walking over to the backdoor, he wiped off his sweat and greeted a few of the regulars who came in almost every day.

"Hey there, Chris! Still going to that college?" said one of the women who was sitting on a long blue mat that traveled across the back wall. It looked like she and her partner, a lithe man with whipcord-like muscles, were stretching out before they sparred.

"Of course. I can't really afford to quit now that I'm in my sophomore year," Chris said. "Besides, becoming a Catgirl Doctor has been my goal since elementary school."

"I still don't understand what a guy like you would want to be a catgirl doctor for," said her partner, shaking his head.

Chris just offered him a polite smile. "I have my reasons."

"Well, whatever you say." The man shrugged.

"Good luck with your schooling," the woman said.

The two heading for the sparring ring after they finished their stretches. Chris went into the backroom, traveled down the hallway toward the men's changing room, and reached his locker. He took out his gym bag, grabbed a towel, and journeyed to the showers, where he stripped his clothes off and took a thorough shower to rid himself of the reek of sweat. After drying off, he wrapped the towel around his waist and began walking back to his locker.

He caught of his reflection in a mirror on the way. Chris ran an absent hand through his messy brown hair as he stared into his own brown eyes. Because he didn't spend much time outdoors, his skin was a bit pale, but he had broad shoulders, a muscular chest, and thick arms. He was nowhere close to Tanner's muscular build. However, Chris couldn't say he was dissatisfied with his current physical condition. He'd worked very hard to gain the strong chest and defined abdominal muscles that he currently possessed.

Slipping on his jeans, a black T-shirt that had the image of a red-haired foxgirl in the front with the words *"Lilian in the streets"* and a raven-haired foxgirl in the back with the words *"Iris in the sheets"* underneath each image, and a water resistant black and red jacket with a hood, Chris slung his gym bag and backpack over his shoulder, and traveled back into the kickboxing center's main area. He waved goodbye to a few people, promised Tanner he'd be around tomorrow, and stepped outside.

It was raining.

The weather is San Diego, California was fairly cold at present. He looked up at the clouds covering the sky, felt the rain beating down on his cheeks, and sighed. It was only a light drizzle right now. However, it was perfectly possible that he'd get caught in a downpour if he didn't hurry home.

Deciding to take a few shortcuts, Chris began cutting through alleys.

Chris lived in Chula Vista, the second largest city in the San Diego metropolitan area. It was given this name because of its scenic location between the San Diego Bay and coastal mountain foothills. Chula Vista actually meant beautiful view in English.

Cutting through Memorial Park, Chris ran across the wet grass, ignoring the way his shoes sank into the soft loam. Thanks to the rain, there wasn't anyone present. It must have started raining at least an hour ago. He glanced at the park way community center, easily visible against the green backdrop of the trees and grass thanks to its blue roofs. Then he turned toward a small bridge located several dozen yards to his left.

He stopped running.

There was a body lying underneath the bridge. He couldn't tell from this distance, but the figure was small, possibly a child. What immediately struck him like a bolt of lightning was the fact that, whoever this person was, it looked like they were wearing rags.

Chris changed direction, racing toward the figure instead of his apartment. He slowed down when he arrived, unsure of what to do before approaching the figure slowly.

"Hey, um, are you okay?"

The figure didn't respond.

As he got closer, Chris noticed several very distinct features on this person, namely, the pure white tail sticking out of what he now recognized as a threadbare blanket and the cat ears on their head. This person was a catgirl. She was lying on her stomach, eyes closed and mouth partially open. He glanced at her face, surrounded by threads of long white hair caked in mud. Her pale skin was smudged with dirt. Even so, he could see a dark bruise forming around her left eye and some scratches on her cheeks.

A chill entered his heart as something slowly closed around it like an icy fist. Kneeling before the girl, he reached out and pressed two fingers to her neck, which was more easily accessible than her wrist right now. *Thump... thump thump... thump.* Her pulse was very weak and her body was freezing cold. He didn't know how long she'd been outside like this, or what had happened, but given her injuries and the temperature of her body, she was in danger of suffering hypothermia. Her body was losing heat faster than it could produce it.

Chris only spent a moment debating on what he should do. He reached into his jacket pocket and pulled out his smartphone. In a situation like this, it was imperative to call Catgirl Rescue Services or the nearest Catgirl Hospital. However, when he tried to turn on his phone, he saw a large flashing symbol of a battery without power.

He cursed. Of all the times for his phone to run out of battery! Thinking about it, he had noticed this morning that his phone hadn't been connected to the charger. He must have forgotten to charge it last night.

"No choice," he muttered.

Chris turned the catgirl over. As her body rolled onto its back, the raggedy blanket fell away, revealing that she was naked underneath it. Chris felt his teeth grinding against each other as he saw how her ribcage was visible. Not only was she malnourished, but there were several bruises covering her body. He had no idea what had happened to her, but he was quick to create a theory that she'd run away from an extremely abusive home.

Acting with care, Chris took off his jacket and wrapped it around the girl, then wrapped the threadbare blanket around her. Next he slipped an arm underneath her legs and his other arm around her shoulders. As he stood to his feet, the girl's legs swung back and forth. He glanced at them. Her feet were covered in scratches and cuts.

He closed his eyes. An overwhelming intense redness had coated his vision, and he needed to take several deep breaths to calm down. Once his emotions were settled, he left the sanctity of the bridge, traveled into the rain, and raced toward his apartment.

There were a lot of things he needed to do, but the first and most important one was to get back home.

chapter 2

Chris's apartment complex was one of several in this area. Shaped like a large J, the complex was four-stories high. There was a small parking lot next to it, but Chris didn't drive so he'd never spent much time there. The area surrounding his complex had a sort of Mediterranean feel. He was sure part of that was because of the grass and palm trees dotting the courtyard.

The rain had gotten much heavier, creating a downpour that pelted him and the catgirl in his arms. He looked at the shivering girl. His expression hardened as he raced through the park, past the pool, his feet sloughing through the wet grass as he forewent the sidewalk to reach the entrance faster. He nearly slipped, but he quickly caught himself and continued. Chris barely even paused as he launched himself up a set of small stairs three at a time, entered the lobby, and ran through it without pausing.

There was no one in the lobby as he ran. Everyone was probably in their apartments, gazing at the rain from their windows or watching TV.

Chris's apartment was on the second floor, and so he raced up a set of stairs, foregoing the elevator because it took too much time. The catgirl in his arms was so cold her lips had turned blue. Bluish coloration of the skin could signal a lack of oxygen to the blood, or it could indicate an abnormal form of hemoglobin, such as in sickle cell anemia. The process of oxygen circulating poorly through the blood caused this bluish discoloration and was referred to as Cyanosis.

The sound of Chris's feet pounding against the floor echoed across the hallway. Several people shouted at him to quiet down through their doors, but no one was willing to actually leave their apartments. Chris ignored them and turned a corner before reaching his apartment, room 243.

Despite being freezing cold, his body was covered in both rainwater and sweat. He breathed heavily as he fumbled for his keys, which were in the jacket he had wrapped around the catgirl. Chris actually had to kneel and place the girl on his thigh, letting her lean against his chest, so he could work his way into his pocket and pull out his keys. Opening the door was also a difficult matter, but he eventually managed to open the door, walk inside, and shut it behind him. With a heavy sigh, he locked the door with a click, then proceeded to his bedroom.

His floor plan was a one-bedroom apartment with a living room, kitchen, bedroom, and bath. Almost immediately after entering, he walked past the kitchen on his left, turned into a small inlet that led to two doors. He took the one on his left again, which opened into a bedroom.

Chris barely paid his decorations any mind as he raced toward the bed. His first thought was to put her on the bed, but then he realized she was wet. If he set her on the bed while she was soaking like this, the water would just soak into the sheets and she would remain cold, which wasn't his purpose. After this thought occurred to him, he thought about what he should do for a moment, then gently placed her on the ground and rushed into his bathroom.

Coming back into the bedroom after grabbing a set of towels, Chris hurriedly removed his jacket and the ragged blanket she had been using to cover herself. She was now completely naked, which meant her bruises and malnutrition body were exposed. While the sight caused him to see red again, he didn't let himself get caught up in his own anger at her condition and instead focused on drying her off.

The temperature in his apartment was set at 80 degrees, but despite that being decently warm, the catgirl was still shivering. He bit his lip. Should he turn up the temperature? No, it would take too long for the temperature to rise.

He finished drying her off, starting from her hair and ears. A catgirl's ears helped regulate their body temperature and should always be warm to the touch. Her ears were cold. Not only that, but as Chris dried them off, he noticed they were covered in grime, dirt, and were slightly blue instead of a healthy pink. That could partially be due to the lack of blood circulating through them, but it might also be a bigger issue. Chris couldn't say for sure unless he gave her a more thorough examination. However, now was not the time.

Once she was dry, Chris lifted her into his arms again, pulled the covers of his bed back, and set her down. He didn't immediately pull the covers back up. First he went to his closet and pulled out an electric heating blanket made from fleece. It was soft to the touch. His fingers brushed through the thick fabric as he clutched it in his hands and went back to the bed. He placed the blanket over her body, making sure she was nice and snug, then turned it on.

He kept the setting low because he didn't want her body getting too hot too quickly. It was better if she gradually warmed up. After that was done, he took a look at her feet.

They were quite small. Her toes were positively tiny, though she had surprisingly pronounced arches. He was sure they'd normally be quite cute, but currently, her feet were covered in tiny lacerations. It looked like she'd cut her feet while running barefoot for who knew how long.

While Chris had many questions, he knew that the most important thing was helping this girl, so he went into his bathroom again and pulled out his first-aid kit. The box was a lot bigger than a normal first-aid kit. It was heavier too. Yet he easily lugged the thing into the bedroom, set it on the floor, and opened it up. Aside from the standard bandages and antiseptics, his first aid kit also had various medical tools like a stethoscope, and several types of medicine and vaccines that were not meant for human use.

Chris only grabbed the bandaids, a wash cloth, and antiseptic right now. He sat down on the bed, right next to the catgirl's feet. The soft foam of the tempur-pedic mattress conformed to his shape as he used an alcohol-based hand sanitizer to clean his own hands. Then he used the washcloth in conjunction with the antiseptic to clean her feet off. He was using a non-alcohol based antiseptic so it wouldn't cause any pain. After removing the grime and blood, he took another antiseptic, this one gel-based, and used his fingers to dab it on and cover the wounds. Finally, he wrapped her feet in bandaids. By the time he was done, the girl's feet were practically covered entirely in skin-colored band aids.

He wasn't quite sure how long this process had taken, but when he looked at the digital clock on his desk, he found that it was 4:30 in the afternoon. He had left the kickboxing center at 3:00 and it normally only took 30 minutes to reach his apartment.

Grrggle!

Chris blinked when his stomach began rumbling. He hadn't eaten since lunch. After briefly considering making himself something to eat, Chris realized he should first clean off. He was covered in rain water and sweat.

Pulling the thermal blanket over the catgirl's feet, Chris then covered her with a regular blanket to help warm her up more. When he got a good look at her face, he saw that the color had returned to her lips, meaning oxygen and blood were circulating through her normally again. Cold temperatures could sometimes cause blood vessels to narrow, leading to temporarily blue-tinged skin. That seemed to be the case here, which was honestly a relief. Chris didn't know what he would have done if she had a more serious problem.

Grabbing his soaking wet jacket, Chris removed his phone and set it on a phone charger that looked like a magic circle. As the phone charger lit up, showing that his phone was now charging, he traveled back into the bathroom.

The first thing he did was take off his shoes and socks. They were soaking wet. And covered in mud. He grimaced when he realized there was likely a trail of mud and water on his carpet now. Sighing, he removed the rest of his clothes, set them on the counter next to his sink, and walked into the bathing area. He shut the door behind him and turned on the water.

It took a moment for the water to heat up, but when it did, he stepped under the warm spray, pressed his hands against the wall, and leaned forward, letting the hot droplets pelt his back. A groan nearly slipped from his mouth as he finally found his tense muscles relaxing.

As he relaxed underneath the water, Chris gave himself a moment to reflect on the past hour and a half. He'd discovered an injured and unconscious catgirl, taken her home, and treated her injuries. However, he still had so many questions his mind felt like it was spinning. Who was she? Where did she come from? What was she doing underneath that bridge?

It was obvious to him that she was a runaway. Merely judging from the bruises on her body and her malnutrition figure, he could easily conclude that her guardian was a horrible human being who had abused her to their heart's content. That much was obvious. Now the only questioned remained was what he should do about it.

The first and most obvious thing he needed to do was contact the authorities. Catgirl abuse was a felony. Depending on the severity of the situation, a person who was caught abusing a catgirl could be punished by incarceration for several years, or life imprisonment without parole. Cases of catgirl abuse were taken incredibly seriously, perhaps more so than cases of regular abuse with humans due to how often catgirl abuse happened.

But before he contacted the authorities, he wanted to make sure the catgirl was okay. Given what happened, she would probably be very frightened when she woke up in a strange apartment with a man she didn't know, and he wouldn't blame her. He needed to make sure she felt safe and comfortable. Then he could contact the proper authorities.

After taking a shower, Chris felt refreshed as he slipped on simple sweat pants and, after a moment's thought, a plain white T-shirt. He normally preferred not wearing shirts around his own place. However, he didn't want the catgirl getting the wrong idea when she woke up. If he woke up and was greeted by a stranger without a shirt, he'd probably assume that person was a sexual predator or something. That was the last thing he wanted.

He headed into the kitchen and rummaged through his fridge and pantry for ingredients. What should he make today? Chris preferred eating hearty meals with lots of meat and bold flavors, but the catgirl would likely not be able to eat such a dish. It could cause stomach problems if she ate something too filling after going so long without a decent meal… which meant he should make something lighter.

As he stared into his fridge, he glanced at the packet of salmon sitting on the middle shelf, an idea coming to him. He decided to make simple pan-seared salmon. Catgirls loved fish. What's more, the combination of protein, omega-3 fatty acids, and vitamin D made it a healthy choice that would help fill her up while not putting stress on her body's ability to break down the food.

Pan-seared salmon was also very easy to make. He preheated a skillet for about 3 minutes, coated the salmon in olive oil before placing it on the skillet, then increased the heat to high. It only took about 8 to 9 minutes total to cook, and he sprinkled capers, salt, and pepper onto the salmon for taste. Once the fish was done browning, he tested it with a fork, watching with a smile as it easily flaked. It was done.

He made three servings of salmon, placing two on one plate and the last on another plate. He garnished them with lemons, then made his way to the small table in his living room and sat down.

Chris thought about turning on the TV. He had a really nice 86 inch LG TV sitting on a gray stand with a built in fireplace. However, while the idea of watching Netflix sounded appealing (He'd heard they had recently added *Evangelion*), Chris wanted to make sure he could hear when the catgirl was waking up. He decided not to turn the TV on, though he did turn on the fireplace. It was remote activated too.

He ate his meal in silence, enjoying the simple flavor of his dish. He'd never call himself a professional chef. That said, he was able to at least make simple dishes and could follow directions well enough not to muck things up. Some of the girls he'd dated had praised his ability to cook, though he was certain they were just impressed he actually could cook. Most of the guys he knew didn't make their own meals.

As he finished eating and was placing his plate in the dishwasher, a loud scream suddenly echoed out from his room.

"MREOW!!!!"

He jolted and rushed over to his room. Chris tried to calm down his racing heart. He was prepared to come in and find a catgirl on the verge of panic, to attempt to calm the girl down and get her to relax so she could eat in peace. That was his only concern as he raced into the bedroom.

Chris did indeed find a catgirl on the verge of panic, huddling up near the corner of the room and staring at her surroundings with wide eyes. She was still covered in the thermal blanket. However, even with that thing covering her, the intense shaking from fear was easy to see. As she looked around, her eyes finally locked with his.

Her eyes were heterochromatic. One was a vibrant blue, while the other looked like gold.

"Uh…"

He froze. What the hell was he supposed to say in a situation like this?

"Um… hello?"

Chris almost groaned at his idiotic greeting. He clearly wasn't winning any awards for eloquence. Really? Couldn't he have at least come up with a more suitable method of saying hi? This wasn't going to ease the catgirl's fear at all.

The catgirl stared at him, not speaking or attempting to move away from that corner, which he noted was the corner furthest from the door. He wondered if he should approach her, but then thought better of it. She might assume he was attacking her and panic even more.

Finally, after what felt like several hours but was probably only minutes, the catgirl spoke.

"Who… are you?"

Her voice was soft and delicate, the kind of gentle, lyrical voice he'd expect from a professional singer.

"My name is Chris Redford," he introduced himself.

"Chris… Red… ford…" the catgirl said his name as though testing it out. Her nose wiggled a little as she spoke and her ears twitched. It was awfully cute, but he knew now wasn't the time to gush.

"I'm sure you're confused," Chris said, and the catgirl focused on him again. Like most catgirls, her pupils looked like slits instead of rounded human pupils. "I don't know exactly what happened to you. I found you unconscious underneath a bridge. You were wet and freezing, so I brought you here."

"Here? Where is… here?" asked the catgirl.

"My apartment," he answered. "It's just a little ways from the bridge I found you under." He paused as the catgirl considered this. "In either case, I'm sure this situation must be frightening. You're in an unknown apartment with someone you've never met, so, er, I'll understand if you don't trust me, but… Oh! I have food! Hold on a moment."

The catgirl's eyes trailed after Chris as he walked out of the bedroom. He came back seconds later with the plate of salmon. When she noticed the plate, her expression perked up. Her nose twitched several times as the scent wafted over to her.

Perhaps it was the scent of the salmon, but the girl tentatively began moving. She kept the blanket wrapped around her body to protect her modesty from him. This actually told Chris a bit more about her. She obviously understood concepts like modesty, which meant she hadn't grown up in an abusive household. Did that mean whoever she had run away from was a new guardian? He didn't know. He hoped to find out what happened to her eventually though.

Finally, the catgirl stopped when she was just a foot or two away from him. She eyed the plate in his hands with a hungry gaze, but then she looked up at him again, and her eyes became cloudy. He guessed she was conflicted. The food smelled delicious, and she clearly wanted to eat it, but there was a strange man handing it to her. She must have been suspicious.

"I'll just leave it here." Chris set the plate down and stood up. "When you're finished eating, you can come into the living room whenever you're ready."

Chris left the bedroom and closed the door behind him, giving the girl some privacy. He went over to his couch, turned on the TV, and lowered the volume. After skimming through Netflix for a little while, he selected a show to watch. His original thoughts had been to turn on *Evangelion*. However, he decided not to right now. What he needed wasn't an anime that would mind fuck him, but some background noise that would help him think. That was why he chose a series called *Tiger & Bunny* instead.

As the show about a veteran hero called Wild Tiger and his new partner Bunny began playing, Chris considered his next options.

Of course, he needed to call the authorities as soon as possible, but his phone was still charging and it was in his bedroom. He thought it would be better not to go inside there right now. There was a branch of the Catgirl Protection Bureau at every police station now, so he wouldn't need to make more than one call.

"I guess, the first thing I should do is learn about her circumstances…" he muttered to himself.

At that moment, a soft clicking sound echoed over to him. He turned his head moments before the catgirl walked out of his bedroom. Her bare feet padded along the carpet. She still had the thermal blanket wrapped tightly around her body. He glanced at the chord and controller dangling from the bottom. The blanket wasn't exceedingly big, but the girl wasn't very tall either. She was maybe 5'1" or 5'2". As he looked at her feet covered in bandages, he once more felt anger at her situation and the person who abused her.

He shunted those emotions aside and smiled at her.

"Are you feeling better now?" The girl nodded once but didn't speak. Chris considered his options for a moment, then patted the spot beside him. "Would you like to take a seat?"

The catgirl looked at the spot he was patting, then glanced at him. The spot. Him. Then the spot again. After a moment, she slowly walked over and sat down. However, Chris noticed that when she sat, it was about as far from him as she could. With her ears twitching periodically, the catgirl curled her knees into her chest, toes clenching against the fabric of the couch as if she was nervous.

As he glanced at the blanket, Chris realized this was going to get awkward for him if he let this girl stay naked the whole time, so he went into his room under her watchful eyes. He checked the battery on his phone. It wasn't even halfway charged. With a grimace, he went through his drawer, pulled out some flannel pajama pants and a large shirt. The pants were dark green while the shirt was white. It had the image of a blue-haired man, drawn in the traditional anime style of artwork and pointing at the sky. He traveled back into the living room and placed the articles of clothing on the modern-looking coffee table that sat in front of the couch.

"Why don't you get dressed?" he suggested.

The catgirl hesitated for a moment, but as he sat back down, she slowly removed the blanket from around her body, reached out and grabbed the pants first. She stood up, stepped into them, and slid them up her hips. Then she threw the shirt over her shoulder. It looked even larger on her than he expected, but when he considered how small and thin she was, he realized it would look way bigger than normal. She wasn't like the girls he'd dated who would sometimes wear his shirts as PJs.

As she sat back down, Chris decided to ask the first question he could think of him.

"Can I… ask your name?"

"… It's Silva," she said.

"Silva…"

As he said her name, Chris couldn't help but wonder if her name was in reference to her white hair, which did look silver when the light reflected off it, though it was hard to tell considering how dirty it was.

Maybe he should give her a bath first… but no. He didn't think she'd trust him enough for that.

"I'm guessing you've been through a really hard time," he said instead. "I assume your guardian mistreated you a lot. Do you… want to talk about it? Tell me what happened?"

Silva bit her lip, sharp canines poking out, then came to a decision.

"I used to have a really nice guardian," she said at last. "Grams. She always treated me well, and I really loved her… but she got old and died. I ended up in an orphanage and was bought by a new guardian. I, um, I don't know how long ago that was. The new guardian seemed really nice at first, but when I got to his home…"

A shiver suddenly ran through her body and she hugged herself. Chris clenched his hands to keep himself from going over to comfort her. The presence of a random stranger would only invoke fear in her. Catgirls did not respond well to strangers. The fact that she was even talking to him was miraculous.

"He locked me up in his basement with several other catgirls. He wasn't nice. He barely fed us and only took us out from the basement to have sex with us. Everyone would always come back down with new bruises and crying. I wasn't taken out very often because Kuro protected me. One day, he came home drunk, and he was really mad about something. He began hitting us really hard. It really hurt."

As he listened to her story, the rage came back. And it brought friends. He didn't let any of his feelings show on his face, however. Chris had enough self-discipline for that. He told himself that his anger would only make Silva fearful of him, that it wouldn't help her.

"B-Big Sister Kuro attacked him and told us all to run. I was really, really frightened, but I listened to her. I ran out of the basement as fast as I could. There was shouting, and screams, and then I heard gunshots. I don't know what happened because I just kept running." As she spoke, her eyes welled up with tears. "I ran and ran and ran. I was so scared. I don't know what happened to Big Sister Kuro or anyone else. I just want to know if they're okay."

As Silva began openly crying, Chris closed his eyes and pieced together what she told him.

Silva had been adopted by a man who had adopted several catgirls before her. That meant he had a license because only someone with one could adopt a catgirl, but while he appeared kind on the surface, that was just a smokescreen. He adopted catgirls and turned them into sex slaves.

Chris didn't know what his reasons for doing this were. Maybe he had a catgirl fetish and just wanted to fuck them, maybe he enjoyed the feelings of power he could lord over them, maybe he was just incredibly twisted, or maybe it was a combination of all three. At the very least, he was obviously a sick and very disturbed individual.

He would need to call the authorities at the first opportunity, but for now, what he needed to focus on was soothing the crying catgirl in front of him.

chapter 3

Silva eventually cried herself to sleep on the sofa. Chris figured she needed it, so he'd silently endured listening to her wails and waited for her to fall asleep before lifting her into his arms. She was incredibly light, though this didn't necessarily surprise him, given that she looked like she hadn't been given anywhere near enough food. The thought caused him to frown. He was going to need to buy her dietary supplements…

Her legs swayed back and forth as he carried the girl back into his bedroom, placed her on the bed, and pulled up the covers. He stood back. Staring at the girl's face, he noticed that her face and hair and probably everything else was still covered in mud and grime. While some of it had been cleaned off when he dried her, the fact remained that she would need to take a bath…

He shook his head. Those were thoughts for another time.

Checking his phone, Chris smiled as he noticed the battery was completely charged, but the smile left when he noticed the time. It was 9:00pm. The Police Department was open 24 hours a day, seven days a week, so he could call them even at this time. However, did he really want police coming to his apartment this late at night? Also, was Silva ready to face the police?

Looking back at the catgirl sleeping on his bed, he debated on what to do. Call the police tonight or wait until tomorrow? He tapped his finger against his phone, but eventually decided he should wait until the next day. Chris was sure whatever would happen when he called the police, it would be an all-day affair, and he wanted to let Silva know about his plans first.

He'd have to let Professor Shinomiya know about what was happening as well. He might even need to call Tanner depending on how the situation developed.

Grabbing a set of spare blankets from his closet, Chris made his way into the living room, placed his smartphone on the coffee table, and laid down on the couch. He used one of the pillows to rest his head. Wrapping himself up in the blanket, Chris fell closed his eyes and tried to fall asleep…

***

A loud beeping startled Chris awake. He fumbled for his phone, groping around, only to frown when he couldn't find it. Blinking his eyes open, he looked around before finding his phone buzzing across the glass top as it vibrated. He reached out and brought the device to his face, shutting off the alarm and glancing at the time.

6:30am.

Rubbing his face, Chris tried to make himself wake up, but hit body felt a lot more sluggish than usual. Well, he would have been shocked if he wasn't at least a bit tired after everything that had happened last night.

A glance at the sliding door leading to his balcony revealed the sun rising across the sky, painting the early morning in the colors of dawn. He looked at the red and pink streaks before turning his gaze to the living room. It had been a long time since he'd slept on the couch like this, though his usual reasons for sleeping on the couch were because he'd pulled an all-nighter playing the latest MMO or watching late-night anime.

Speaking of reasons for sleeping on the couch…

Chris made his way to the bedroom and took a peek inside, breathing a sigh of relief when he found Silva still sleeping on his bed. He hadn't really been worried, per say, but given what happened… well, okay. He actually was a little worried. Chris feared the girl would have had night terrors over what happened, but she seemed okay.

He closed the door again, made his way into the kitchen, and began cooking some scrambled eggs. The eggs were lightly seasoned with salt and pepper. After serving them up on a plate, he added some shredded cheese and Tabasco sauce.

Sitting down at the table, he slowly ate his meal and considered his course of action. First, he needed to wake up Silva, have her eat breakfast, and let her take a bath. Second, he needed to call the police while she was taking a bath. Third, he needed to call Professor Shinomiya and let her know he might not be able to make it for classes. His actions after that would largely depend on how his meeting with the police went.

Once everything was settled in his mind, Chris put his plate in the dishwasher, traveled back into his room—and paused.

He sniffed the air once.

His nose wrinkled.

Something smelled *awful*. It was like someone had taken month old dirty socks, put rotten eggs in them, then soaked the socks in formaldehyde. He'd never smelled something quite like this.

As he was wondering where that smell was coming from, he walked up to the bed, which only made the scent stronger. That was when he realized it was actually coming from the girl.

He glanced down at Silva, who was still peacefully sleeping. Her nose wiggled a few times. However, she must have been quite exhausted because she was still asleep.

Now that he was thinking about it, Chris should have realized Silva hadn't taken a bath in a long time. He would bet money that Silva's previous guardian had not let her take a bath except when he was going to use her. How many days had she gone without a bath? He didn't know. However, it was certainly more than a weak. The reason he hadn't been able to smell her last night was likely due to a combination of the situation overriding his sense of smell and the rain water temporarily washing it away.

Trying his best to ignore the stench, he reached out and gently shook Silva by the shoulder. She didn't stir at first. However, when she eventually opened her eyes, they did so with a wide snap. Instantly locking eyes with him, Silva released a terrified shriek and leapt out of the bed.

"Whoa!"

Chris stumbled back as the girl landed on the other side in a crouch and shot toward the corner, where she quickly assumed a terrified defensive posture, the same one she'd been in last night.

"Easy there, Silva," he said, making sure to call her by name. "It's just me. It's Chris. Remember?"

"Chris?" Silva blinked several times as she stared at him, then gradually relaxed. He sighed in relief when the shaking stopped entirely. "I remember you."

"Good." He sighed in relief. "Anyway, I'm going to make you some breakfast. In the meantime, I think you should take a bath."

"A bath?" Silva suddenly stiffened.

"Yes…" Chris nodded as he eyed the girl with a guarded look. "Have you not taken a bath before?"

"I have," she quickly assured him. "My previous guardian would take baths with me. I always liked the warm water. It's just…"

When the girl trailed off with an embarrassed blush, a horrible feeling came over Chris. There was something about the way she spoke that forced him to realize a startling truth.

"You've never taken a bath without your guardian before, have you?" he asked. She shook her head. "Do you think you can do so now?" She paused, then shook her head again, causing him to sigh. "Then… would you like to take a bath with me?"

He honestly wasn't sure he approved of the idea of taking a bath with this catgirl. He didn't know how old she was, but he just felt like there was something wrong about the whole thing. However, she really did need a bath, and if she couldn't take one on her own, then he'd have to suck it up and deal with the situation.

"Yes, please," Silva said in a soft voice.

And that was how Chris ended up in the bath, half-naked because he didn't want his shirt getting wet. He refused to remove his pants since he wasn't planning to hop in the bath with her.

His bathtub wasn't what he would call big, but it could probably fit two people if they squeezed in. It had a detachable showerhead, which he was making great use of at the moment to wet her hair. Silva's eyes were squinted shut as she bore with the feeling of water droplets raining down on her. Her tail was bristling and her ears periodically twitched.

Once she was thoroughly wet, the first thing Chris did was wash her hair. He didn't have any special shampoo and conditioner for catgirls, so he had to make do with the stuff he used. He started at the ends, working the shampoo into her hair before slowly moving up. As he worked, Chris took care not to injure her, applying only a light pressure as he massaged her scalp.

"You're really good at this," Silva muttered, her voice slightly astonished.

"Well, I have a catgirl back home," he admitted. "I found her when I was just a child and convinced my parents to become her guardians. She's about the same age as me, and we often took baths together. I learned how to wash a woman's hair from washing her hair."

"So you already have a catgirl..." Silva wore a very small frown at that, then cracked her left eye open a bit to look at him. "Is this not your home?"

"It is temporarily," he answered. He'd finished lathering up her hair and was now using the showerhead to thoroughly rinse it. "Keep your eyes closed please." When Silva shut her eyes, he continued talking. "I'm currently attending college here to be a Catgirl Doctor. San Diego State University has the best courses for people who want to become Catgirl Doctors at the moment, so I ended up moving away from home."

"Will you move back?" asked Silva.

"Probably temporarily. I promised Elsa that I would come back to pick her up once I graduated."

Chris paused as he finished washing her hair, trying to withhold a snort at the sight of Silva's long locks covering her entire front like Cousin It. He reached out and moved her hair away from her face, twisting it into a slight twirl that he could move as needed to wash the rest of her body. He used regular wash soap to clean her body, getting her arms, back, armpits, chest, stomach, legs, and feet, then used the showerhead to rinse it all away.

"She sounds important," Silva said.

"She is very important," Chris agreed before turning off the showerhead and standing up. "Okay. You're all done. Let's dry you off."

Silva stood up, dripping wet as she stepped out of the bath and onto the bath mat. Chris grabbed a pair of towels. He wrapped one around her hair, then used the other to dry her off. Silva let him do as he needed. She didn't seem too concerned that he might try something, which he found a little odd, but maybe she had simply decided to trust him... or maybe she'd been so abused that she didn't see anything wrong with their situation.

He shook his head before his thoughts could take another dark turn and stepped back.

"Could you stand here in front of the mirror please?" he requested.

Silva did as she was instructed. Chris then removed the hair towel and began using a blow dryer in conjunction with a brush to comb and dry her hair. Just like when he was washing her hair, he started from the ends and worked his way up, combing and drying at the same time.

Under his ministrations, Silva seemed to melt. Her body slackened, her eyes glazed over, and her lips curled into a blissful smile. It was the first smile he'd seen on her, and he had to admit that it was rather pretty. Chris wondered what was contained within that smile. Perhaps she was remembering better times with her previous guardian.

Finally, Silva was clean and dry, so Chris rummaged through the drawers in his bedroom and pulled out a pair of sweatpants and a T-shirt. Once again, the red sweatpants were far too large on her tiny frame, but they could be adjusted using the drawstrings while the bottoms were rolled up so she wouldn't trip, and Chris tied his shirt into a knot near the back so it would stop sliding off. Once she was dressed, he asked her to sit down at the dinner table and made her an omelet with bacon bits, cheese, and some vegetables thrown in.

"It's a pretty simple meal, but I hope you like it," Chris said as he set down a plate and fork in front of Silva.

Silva looked at the fork for a moment, then clumsily took it into her hand and started eating. Chris frowned for a moment, shook his head, then sat down at the other end of the table. He felt a little creepy just watching her eat. However, he wanted her to finish eating before he said anything further, and she didn't really seem bothered, though he took that with a grain of salt right now.

"I'm thinking of calling the police and letting them know about what happened to you," he said only after Silva had cleaned off her plate. The catgirl perked up, silver ears twitching as she stared at him, prompting Chris to continue. "Catgirl abuse is a serious offense, and it sounds like this guy has been abusing catgirls for a long time now. I'll need to let the police know what happened. However, when I call them, it is likely that you'll need to give them an accounting of what happened to you. Is that something you're okay with?"

Silva bit her lip, once more causing her cute fangs to poke out of her mouth. Chris waited patiently for her to say something.

"I… I think that's a good idea. Um, if you call the police, I'll tell them what happened to me."

"Okay." Chris sighed and ran a hand through his hair. "Then that's what we'll do."

With Silva's words cementing his decision, Chris got out his smartphone and dialed 911…

***

"It sounds like you've gotten yourself into a really serious predicament," Professor Shinomiya said from the other side of the phone.

"I can't deny that." Chris ran a hand through his hair. "Anyway, I just wanted to call you to let you know why I won't be attending classes today."

"I understand. This is a wise choice. However, since you won't be at school, I recommend asking someone like Ms. Anastasia Pierce for her notes when you see her."

"I'll be sure to do that."

"Take care."

As Professor Shinomiya hung up, Chris removed the smartphone from his ear and glanced at Silva. She was sitting on the couch, wearing his clothes that were far too big for her, knees drawn up to her chest as she watched cartoons on the TV.

A glance at the TV revealed she was watching *My Roommate is a Cat*. It was a series about a novelist who was shy and struggled to form relationships with other people, and a cat who had been abandoned by humans and forced to live on the streets. Through some twist of fate, they end up living together. It was very much a fluffy slice-of-life show. Not really something he was into.

He sat down on the couch as well, making sure he sat on the other side so as not to frighten Silva. She didn't even seem to be paying attention, however. Her eyes were glued to the screen, sparkling as she watched the interactions between Mikazuki and his cat roommate.

"I called the police," Chris said after a few moments of silence. Silva's ears twitched. "They said they'll arrive in about twenty minutes, so they'll probably be here soon." He paused. Silva had turned her head from the TV to look at him. "Are you sure you're okay with this?"

Silva tilted her head, then slowly nodded. "I... I am. I don't know much about the laws, but I know if something bad happens, you're supposed to go to the police. Grams always told me that."

"Grams?"

"My previous guardian," she elaborated.

"Ah."

So that was what she called her previous guardian. He remembered she had mentioned a "Grams" the night before, but he had been more focused on learning about what she'd been through.

Still, this didn't surprise him. Elsa called his mom and dad "Momma" and "Pappa" as if they were her real parents. Catgirls often formed familial bonds with their guardians— rare exceptions being like the case he found himself in right now—and would take to referring to their guardians by such names.

A knock on his door sounded out moments later, causing Silva to nearly jump off the couch. She eyed the door like it had suddenly transformed into a monster. Chris glanced at her, then stood up and made his way to the door, undoing the locks and opening it.

Two people wearing a long-sleeved black shirt with the badge of the San Diego Police Department on both shoulders and black slacks stood on the other side. The one in front was a woman with dark skin and long hair drawn into a tight bun, while the other person was a woman with pale skin and red hair. On their left breast was another symbol. It was a badge made in the silhouette of a cat head.

"You're the police who've come to investigate the matter regarding Silva?" he asked.

It was clear neither of them knew who Silva was. Their faces showed clear confusion. The person he had spoken to on the other end had been a man, so they might not have all the details. Maybe Silva's name just hadn't been mentioned when the person he spoke to ordered this pair to arrive.

"We're here because we received a report of an abused runaway catgirl being here," the woman said. "I'm officer Jennifer Hudson, and this is my partner Ellen Demire. We're with the Catgirl Protection Bureau. Are you Chris Redford?"

The Catgirl Protection Bureau was a branch of the government that dealt with all catgirl matters. They were also part of the police forces, and it was their job to deal with any cases involving catgirls. Since catgirl abuse and sexual assault were the most common cases they dealt with, this branch was made up primarily of women, since it was judged that a catgirl would feel more at ease talking to a woman than a member of the same gender who abused them. Of course, there were known cases of women abusing catgirls, which was why the bureau wasn't entirely composed of women. Just mostly.

"I am." Chris moved back and opened the door further. "Silva is inside. I assume you want to speak with her?"

"We will in a little bit, but first we'd like to ask you a few questions," Officer Hudson said as she and her partner entered his apartment.

"Okay."

The police glanced around his apartment as they walked inside, but their eyes soon locked onto Silva, who was warily watching them from the couch. My Roommate is a Cat was still playing in the background. However, Silva wasn't even paying a cursory glance to the show anymore as she stared at the two newcomers like they were intruders. Her ears and tail were bristling.

"Can I get you two anything to drink?" Chris asked.

"No, thank you," Officer Demire replied. "It's against regulations to accept drinks from people we are questioning."

"I see. I had no idea."

"There have been known cases where someone has offered members of the Catgirl Protection Bureau drugged drinks," Officer Hudson told him. "Ever since the first case where this happened, the new policy where we aren't allowed to accept drinks or food was put into place."

Chris nodded, but he didn't say anything about that as he led the pair over to his living room table. When they sat down, Chris pulled out his wallet, removed a card from inside, and set it on the table in front of them. It looked like a standard ID. His face, name, address, and all pertinent information were there. However, unlike a normal ID or Driver's License, this had the seal of cat paw imprinted on the left and the words *Catgirl Guardianship License* instead of *Driver's License*.

"I don't know how these incidents work," Chris said with a shrug when the two officers stared at him. "I figured I'd give you my identification first."

While Officer Demire snorted, Officer Hudson smiled.

"We certainly would have asked if you have a Catgirl Guardianship License, but even if you didn't have one, we wouldn't hold that against you," she explained. "From what I understand, you found that catgirl and rescued her. If you didn't have a license, we wouldn't be able to let her stay with you unless you were willing to undergo certification, but we wouldn't arrest you or anything."

"Oh… okay."

Chris felt a bit of heat rushing to his cheeks. He was trying to be as accommodating as possible so this entire process would go smoothly, but maybe he was being too accommodating?

"Anyway, let's get down to the questions," Officer Hudson said, and Chris nodded.

The first few questions they asked mostly pertained to him, what he did for a living, then what college he was going to, followed by what he was attending college for. Both officers expressed surprised when he told them he was training to be a Catgirl Doctor. The questions after asking basic knowledge about him changed to how he had discovered Silva and the events after finding her. When he finished, the expressions on both officers faces had grown quite dark, but there was also gratitude in their eyes.

"It seems that girl really would have died if you hadn't discovered her," Officer Hudson said. "You did a good job."

"Thank you," Chris replied.

"Now we need to question Ms. Silva," Officer Demire said.

Everyone turned to look at Silva. The catgirl had been watching from the couch. When their eyes landed on her, her entire back stiffened and her tail stood straight on end. Her eyes darted back and forth as if looking for a way to escape.

Chris, realizing Silva was still terrified despite her words from before about how she would speak with the police, moved over to the couch and knelt in front of her. Silva's gold and blue eyes locked with his.

"Are you sure you're ready for this?" he asked. Silva hesitated a little before nodding. "Okay. Would you be more comfortable if I left?" She shook her head. It was an immediate response. "All right. I'll stay right here."

Chris sat down next to Silva, who must have been extremely nervous because she shifted so close to him that their thighs touched. He imagined she was not comfortable around two more strangers. Between the more familiar presence and these two new ones, she wanted to be closer to him than them.

The two police officers stood up. While Officer Demire hung in the back, Officer Hudson knelt on the floor like Chris had done and gave Silva a reassuring smile.

"Don't worry," she said. "I understand your nervous. Feel free to take your time. You can tell us your story whenever you're ready."

Silva still didn't speak. Her tail was bristling and her ears were twitching. Her hands and even her arms and legs were shaking.

When Chris saw this, he hesitated just for a moment before reaching out and grabbing her nearest hand. Her hand was much smaller than his. Now that she had properly washed, her hand was also warm and smooth. Her fingers were small and delicate.

His actions caused Silva to jump. She looked down at his hand, then at his face. After traveling back and forth between his hand and face, she slowly tightened her hand around his, gripping it fiercely. Then her tail miraculously came out from behind her back and curled around his arm.

The officers watching said nothing, but there was an odd look in their eyes that Chris couldn't place.

After that, Silva told them what she had told him the night before. Even though he had already heard the story, Chris could not help but clench his teeth behind closed lips hearing it again. The anger he felt at Silva's mistreatment returned. However, he said nothing and did his best to give no indication about his feelings. Right now, his purpose was to be there for this catgirl who was retelling the events of her abuse.

"I think we have everything," Officer Hudson said as she stood up. Behind her, Officer Demire was returning her smartphone to a holster at her side. She'd been jotting down notes the entire time Silva spoke. "We'll file this report with the Catgirl Protection Bureau and see if we can discover anything about this man. It's unfortunate that we don't have a name, but since we know what he looks like and know that he has a Catgirl Guardianship License, we can search through our database until we find him. I'm sure the bureau will contact you once we have information regarding this case. If we catch this guy, Ms. Silva may need to come and testify against him."

"I understand," Chris said as Silva shuddered at the thought of meeting her abuser again.

"In the meantime, there are a few things we need you to do while the investigation is underway," Officer Hudson began again.

"I need to head to a Certified Catgirl Hospital and have Silva get a checkup, right?" Chris said.

"As expected of a man training to be a Catgirl Doctor," Officer Hudson chuckled. "Yes, you should first get a checkup at a Certified Catgirl Hospital. The nearest one is the Chula Vista Catgirl Clinic. I'll call in and let them know to expect you. Since this is a matter of catgirl abuse, the Catgirl Protection Bureau will also pay for her checkup. Just send us the receipt and we'll reimburse you."

"Okay. I'll take her in today," Chris said.

"Good," Officer Hudson said. "In that case, we'll be on our way."

Chris stood up to see the two officers to the door. However, his hand was still in Silva's, and she was not letting go, so he ended up taking her with him. She traveled behind him, gripping his hand tightly as he walked the officers to his apartment entrance. As they were leaving, Officer Hudson observed him and Silva with a strange look, then smiled.

"You must be an extraordinary individual," she said.

"Huh?" was Chris's eloquent response.

"A lot of catgirls who have been abused find themselves unable to trust in members of the male persuasion," the officer explained. "Some even find it hard to trust in humans altogether and end up in care centers run entirely by catgirls." Officer Hudson pointed at Silva with her chin. "The fact that Silva is so attached to you and trusts you this much after just meeting tells me you must be an incredibly kind and compassionate person."

Chris had never thought of himself as particularly kind or compassionate—at least, no more than any other normal person. At the same time, he would not deny that he had a soft spot for catgirls. There was a reason he had decided to become a Catgirl Doctor.

"Thank you," he said.

Officer Hudson offered him one last smile before disappearing out the door. After he shut the door behind her, locking it, he glanced at the girl beside him.

"Are you okay?" he asked. She nodded. "You were very brave just now." His words caused her to look up, eyes widening in surprise as he scratched his cheek. "But you know, now that it's over, you don't have to be brave anymore if you don't want to be."

His words caused Silva's eyes to tremble. Her lips twisted into an expression filled with pain. It was like she was trying to hold a monster at bay inside of her, but the prison that kept it locked away was crumbling before, finally, it broke.

With a loud cry, Silva lunged forward and slammed into him, knocking Chris back a few steps. Her hands grabbed the back of his shirt as she released a flood of tears that stained his shirt. Chris didn't mind, however. Wrapping one arm around the catgirl's shoulders, he stroked her hair with the other and let Silva cry.

chapter 4

Chris tried not to let his discomfort show as Silva clung to him like a super adorable limpet. She was hugging his arm so tightly he thought the circulation might cut off, all the while gazing at the numerous other people sitting on the bus with them, eyes wary. In return, the many other people on the bus stared at the catgirl with shocked gazes.

Not that he could blame them.

While catgirls were not an unusual sight (in fact, there were two catgirls on the bus right now), Silva's outfit made her stand out. Her sweatpants were several sizes too large. The hems had been rolled up. On her feet were simple flip flops, also too large for her tiny feet. She was wearing a shirt, though it was hidden under the several sizes too big black hoodie. The hoodie was one of his favorites. It featured a girl on the front who looked like an angel and had a bright and cheerful smile curling her lips. She was holding a sci-fi tool of some kind and the words *What should I invent today?* were underneath her image.

Out of the corner of his left eye, he caught one of the catgirls staring at them. Her hair was branded with different colors, though it appeared predominantly orange. Larger than normal ears sat on her head. Judging from her distinctive tabby-colored hair, lithe but tall figure, she was an Abyssinian. When he looked at her, the catgirl's green eyes widened and her pupils shrank as she looked away. The woman she was with, an older woman, glared at Chris like he'd just committed a grave sin.

Now it was Chris' turn to look away.

"Try not to be so nervous," Chris said to Silva. "Take a deep breath and relax. I won't let anything happen to you. I promise."

That seemed to do the trick. Silva took a deep breath, then let it all out, her body relaxing. Yet even though her grip on his arm slackened, she still kept herself glued to his side. He sighed.

It was fortunate that their stop was not too far. The Chula Vista Catgirl Clinic was only twenty minutes away by bus.

Once he saw their stop, he tugged a small chord to let them know someone wanted to get off. When the bus slowed to a stop, he stood, taking Silva with him, and exited the bus.

As the bus drove off, Chris glanced at the Chula Vista Medical Plaza. It was a large building with an asymmetrical design, three-stories high, and not their destination. Still letting Silva hug his arm, he walked to a smaller building sitting right next to it. While the building was smaller, it was also much longer and looked cleaner than the medical plaza. On the front wall next to a sliding glass door were the words Chula Vista Catgirl Clinic.

Chris entered the clinic with Silva. He took a moment to glance at the main lobby, where several catgirls and their guardians were sitting in chairs. A few of the catgirls were coughing or sniffling. Chris noticed how most of them appeared quite young, but there was an older catgirl who was looking after a litter of younger catgirls. After taking a survey of the interior, he went passed the chairs and toward the front desk, where another catgirl was sitting.

"How may I help you two?" asked the catgirl.

Most people would have probably mistaken this catgirl for a child. She was shorter than even Silva, had no breasts to speak of, and a cherubic face. She was a munchkin cat. They were a breed that looked young and small for life. Despite her appearance, the catgirl dressed smartly in a long skirt and collared shirt looked at them with a professionalism that contrasted with her appearance.

"We're here to have a checkup," Chris said as he reached into his pocket with his free hand to pull out his wallet. "My name is Chris Redford. This is Silva. The San Diego Police Department should have called in to let you know we'd be coming."

It took a bit of work to remove his Catgirl Guardianship License from his wallet with only one hand (Silva was still clinging to his other), but he managed it and presented the ID to the munchkin catgirl, whose name tag said she was called Lidia. She read the ID information, typed it into the computer in front of her, and paused for a moment to see if her search pulled up any information.

"Here you two are," she said. "It looks like the police did call in for you. You've been scheduled to meet with Dr. Alice Medisson. She is currently with a patient, but if you fill out this form while you wait, I can let her know you've arrived."

"Thank you," Chris said as he took a small sheet from Lidia. It was attached to a clipboard for easy writing. There were several pens on the desk, so he grabbed one and directed Silva to the chairs.

As they sat down, Chris had to pull his arm free from her grip so he could write the information needed for the form. Silva did not look happy about this, but she didn't fight it either, and instead turned her attention to the other catgirls. Her eyes betrayed a hint of fascination as she watched some of the younger ones from the litter rough-housing. A few of them were rolling around the floor and had to be brought in line by the oldest of the bunch. Chris wondered if the woman belonged to a catgirl orphanage.

The information requested was all standard stuff: Name. Age. Sex. Reason for coming. He filled it out along with the information he had on Silva. Then he stood up and went to the desk to give Lidia the form. Silva reacted to his sudden move with a startled hiss, but when she saw him walking away, she scrambled to her feet and quickly caught up.

"Here you go," Chris said.

"Oh. Thank you." Lidia looked over the form, nodded, and then set it down on the table next to her computer. "I let Dr. Alice Medisson know that you are here. She should be finished with her current patient in just a few moments."

"We understand," Chris said.

They sat back down, silence elapsing between them. When Chris glanced at Silva, he saw that her legs were jumping up and down, hands clenching her sweatpants as she occasionally glanced at him, only to look away again.

He reached out and placed a hand over one of hers.

"I don't think you need to be so jumpy," he said.

"I'm sorry," Silva apologized, shoulders hunching as if trying to hide. "I just… it's been a really long time since I was able to be outside like this. I'm nervous."

Chris would have pointed out that she'd been outside when she escaped from her previous guardian, but he didn't. She'd been on the run at the time. He imagined she barely had time to figure out where she was going, never mind observe her surroundings with any form of clarity. It was only natural that she'd be nervous in a situation like this.

Catgirls were also naturally skittish and prone to disliking changes to their situation.

To keep the girl from being nervous, Chris engaged her in small talk. He didn't know what to talk about, so he simply told her about his college and what he was studying in class.

"My current classes are on catgirl physiology and catgirl psychology. At present, we're mostly focusing on reproduction in physiology. Professor Shinomiya is my teacher in that class. She's pretty strict and hates it when anyone slacks off in her class. She also isn't above kicking people out."

"She doesn't sound like a very nice person," Silva muttered.

Chris chuckled a little. "She is strict, but that's not to say she isn't nice. She's very understanding. When I called and let her know about the situation I'm in, she told me to not worry and to just copy the notes from one of my classmates."

As they were speaking, the doors near the front desk suddenly slid open, admitting three people. One of them was an older man, another was a young catgirl child, and the last was a brown-haired woman wearing a lab coat. The gentleman was thanking the doctor for giving the young catgirl a checkup. After they said goodbye to the doctor, the pair left hand in hand, reminding Chris of a father and his child.

"Chris Redford?" the woman suddenly called out.

"That's me," Chris said.

He stood up and pulled Silva with him. Together, they walked toward the woman, though Silva once again hid behind him.

"I'm Alice Medisson," the woman greeted. Up close, he could see that she was wearing black slacks and a black shirt underneath her lab coat. The slightly cleavage revealing shirt didn't look strictly regulation, but she seemed completely at ease wearing it, so she must be important enough that no one would say anything about it.

"It's a pleasure to meet you," Chris greeted before gesturing to the girl hiding behind him. "This is Silva."

Dr. Medisson took one look at Silva, then her eyes softened. Her lips turned into a gentle smile that seemed both tender and professional.

"I've heard about your circumstances," she said. "I know it might be hard to trust me at first, but do not worry. None of the tests I'm planning to run will hurt. I promise."

Silva glanced suspiciously at the woman before looking at Chris. He smiled and nodded. Silva then looked back at Dr. Medisson.

"It's nice to meet you," Silva said softly.

"Come with me, please." Dr. Medisson offered Silva one last smile before turning back toward the doorway, which was still open. Then she turned just her head and glanced at him. "You're free to come with us as well. In fact, it seems she might be more comfortable with you present."

Chris nodded as he and Silva followed Dr. Medisson into a hallway. They passed several catgirls and humans dressed in lab coats, as well as what looked like a few patients and their families. Dr. Medisson soon turned a corner, then entered the second room on their right, which he and Silva followed her through.

The room was a standard medical examination office. It looked a lot like a human examination office except for several objects that didn't belong in a human office, like the scratching post, balls of yarn, and several other cat-specific objects.

"Please sit down on the examination table," Dr. Medisson instructed as she went over to a counter and grabbed a stethoscope.

Silva did as she was asked, sitting on the table and nervously kicking her legs back and forth Meanwhile, Chris sat down on a chair next to the door.

What happened next was Dr. Medisson running through a series of very standard tests. She listened to Silva's heart, lungs, and intestinal tract with the stethoscope. Then she used a reflex hammer to test Silva's reflexes. Everything seemed fairly normal. However, there were a few tests that catgirls had, which humans did not have.

"Okay. I want you to follow this with your eyes," Dr. Medisson said as she held up a simple cat tail toy. She waved the toy back and forth across Silva's field of vision, and as she did, Silva became entranced, her eyes locking onto the toy as it swung back and forth with a hypnotic motion.

"Meow…"

A low noise issued from Silva's throat. It was something he had never heard from her before, though, granted, it hadn't even been a full 24 hours since they met.

"Meow."

As she followed the toy, her pupils seemed to grown thinner somehow, like when a human's eyes become dilated.

"Mreow!"

Seconds later, Silva pounced. She leapt off the examination table and tried to grab the toy, but Dr. Medisson dodged to the left like an expert. However, Silva didn't give up. She got down on all fours and quickly launched herself at the cat toy like she wanted to rip it to shreds, but even so, the good doctor once again moved the cat toy out of her field of vision. Silva landed on the ground and spun around, ready to attack the toy once again.

"It looks like her instincts are still intact," Dr. Medisson said as she put the toy away and scribbled some notes onto a tablet.

Silva blinked several times as she realized the cat toy was no longer present. She looked around as if still searching for it, then became disappointed upon realizing it was gone.

Because they were doing more than a standard checkup, it wasn't just these basic tests they needed to take. Dr. Medisson directed them to another room where Silva was given a full-body X-ray. She also had Silva walk on a treadmill and breath into an apparatus that tested her heart rate, made her balance on one leg to test her balance, took and a test that checked her vision, etc.

After all the tests were done, Chris and Silva found themselves back in the first medical room they'd used with Dr. Medisson.

"It looks like aside from malnutrition and bruising, Silva is in good condition," Dr. Medisson explained. "She has no broken bones and there's nothing wrong with her physically. However, I do recommend buying dietary supplements for her so she can bring her weight back up to a healthy level. She's grossly underweight by at least twenty pounds."

"The healthy weight for a Khao Manee is between 105 and 115 pounds," Chris said.

Dr. Medisson smiled. "That is correct, and right now, she's only 85 pounds."

"I'll buy some supplements," Chris concluded after a moment. "I know of a good company who makes dietary supplements for catgirls."

"Good. Then it looks like your checkup is concluded." Dr. Medisson smiled. "Congratulations. You're all clear. Let me walk you two out."

Dr. Medisson walked them into the lobby, where Chris and Silva said goodbye. Silva was much more open when she spoke. During the several hour checkup, she seemed to have grown accustomed to the doctor's presence, which either spoke of her strength as an individual or the doctor's skills as a medical professional.

Once they emerged from the Chula Vista Catgirl Hospital, Chris looked at the sky. The sun was high overhead and a brisk breeze was blowing through the streets, creating a slight chill that caused Silva to shudder and wrap her arms around herself.

"Are we going home?" asked Silva.

Chris frowned for a moment, glanced at the clock on his smartphone, and shook his head.

"No. It's about lunch time right now," Chris said. "I think we should grab a bite to eat." He paused to look Silva up and down, or rather, to look at her clothes. "Also, we should buy you some clothes that fit."

Silva's response to his words was to tilt her head.
"Meow?"

***

Chris concluded that Silva must have been to the mall before, because she didn't seem surprised so much as she did frightened. She hugged his arm close again as they were enclosed by a horde of humans and catgirls. A little to his left was a small family of four. Three of them were human, but the last child was a catgirl. To his right, a pair of catgirls were chatting as they walked, their ears twitching as girlish giggling escaped their lips. Perhaps it was because of their distinctive ears, but even though there were far more humans than catgirls (there was at least 20 humans to every catgirl), Chris still found it easier to spot these humanoid felines among the crowd.

He glanced down at the catgirl on his arm and watched as she jumped at laughter to her left, nearly shrieked when a loud shout startled her, and hissed at an older gentleman who almost bumped into her.

"Do you not like crowds?" asked Chris.

Silva glanced up at him, bit her lip, then shook her head. "It isn't that I don't like crowds, or being in crowded places. I guess it's just been so long since I've seen so many people." She paused as her lips trembled. "Am I being a bother?"

"No." Chris shook his head. "You aren't being a bother. I was just wondering."

Since he didn't want her thinking she was annoying him, Chris dropped the subject. He was sure she would become more used to crowds once she got outside more. It would just take time.

Chris's goal in coming to the mall was to find suitable clothes for Silva. Within this mall were three large companies that sold clothes: JCStaff, A-1 Clothing, and Ufotable's. However, there were also small boutiques that sold high end clothing like Kyoto Fashionation, which specialized in Japanese clothing.

He decided to try JCStaff first. Their clothing was what he would call the middle ground. It wasn't as expensive as Ufotable's, but it wasn't cheap like A-1 Clothing.

Because Silva was so small, they went to the children's section to buy clothes. Chris wouldn't lie and say he didn't feel awkward as he helped Silva pick out some underwear and clothing, but he considered it a small price to pay. She needed clothes. That was a fact.

Given her silver hair and small body, he thought having her wear clothes with a more feminine appeal like skirts and dresses suited her better. Dresses were also easier for catgirls to wear because they didn't need to worry about their tail getting trapped. He also grabbed several sets of underwear for catgirls before leading Silva to a series of changing rooms where she could get dressed.

"Just come out when you finish changing into one of these," Chris said. "We'll figure out what to buy after you've tried everything on."

"Okay."

Silva nodded as she accepted the clothes and entered the changing room. Chris almost sighed in relief. It seemed she didn't need him to help her get dressed, which would have been awkward since one of the employees had been staring at him for awhile now. He tried to ignore the stare, but it really did make him uncomfortable.

He listened to the rustling of fabric coming from the other side, then turned around when the door suddenly opened. Silva stood in the doorway. Dressed in a very simple white gown that ended just above the knees, she presented a very lovely picture. Her pale skin and silver hair was complemented by the white dress. Her heterochromatic eyes stood out the most. He glanced down and saw that she was white slipper shoes and pale pink socks.

"Does it look okay?" asked Silva.

"Yeah…" Chris slowly nodded as he found himself approving of her appearance. "I think clothes like this definitely suit you. Could you try on a few more outfits? You'll need more than just one pair of clothes, after all."

Silva nodded, her eyes sparkling a bit more now than they had before. Perhaps being able to shop for clothing was sparking some joy in her. He didn't know if it was the idea of wearing cute clothes, shopping, or something else entirely, but he felt this was a good thing. Up until this point, all Silva had done was stare suspiciously at everyone around them and jump at the slightest noise. He was glad something was exciting her.

She went back into the changing room and dressed in several more outfits. One of them was another dress, but this one was blue with white accents. Another was a mid-thigh length black skirt and white shirt combination. The shirt was one of those shoulder-less numbers that showed off the tops of her shoulders. For her last outfit, she dressed in more boyish clothing.

"Oh?" Chris perked up. "I think this one might suit you the best."

"You think so?"

Silva looked down at her outfit and moved about. The jeans shorts were pretty short. They revealed a lot of her pale legs. On her feet were simple black and white converse. A sleeveless black shirt hung from her shoulders, a bit too big for her, but he'd done that on purpose. She was currently under weight, so he needed to buy clothes that she could wear after reaching a healthy weight.

"I do." Chris grinned. "You look really cute!"

Perhaps it was the enthusiasm in his words, but Silva's eyes widened seconds before all the blood rushed to her cheeks. She looked down. Her ears erratically twitched several times as her tail shot straight into the air. These particular clothes were made with catgirls in mind. There was a hole in the back just above her butt that her tail could slip through.

"Anyway, I think we'll get these outfits for now," he said, nodding to himself. "We'll want to buy some more clothes for you later, but I'd rather wait until you've reached a healthy weight."

"I understand," Silva said. She dithered for a moment. "Should I... change back?"

Chris actually pondered that for a moment before deciding to ask the employee who'd been watching them this whole time. The young woman dressed in the black and red uniform of a JCStaff member looked startled when he came up to her, but when he asked if Silva could wear those out, she told him that it was fine. He just needed to give the cashier the price tags so they could be scanned.

"It's fine," Chris said. "Let's get those price tags off and you can wear those out."

When Silva began beaming like she'd just won the lottery, Chris knew he'd made the right choice.

They were soon standing in front of the cash register as a catgirl scanned their goods. The catgirl working the register was bright and friendly, greeting them with a smile and engaging Silva in a conversation. What made Chris happy was that Silva seemed at ease talking to this random catgirl. He wondered if that was a sign of her slowly becoming less skittish, or if it was just easier to speak with her own kind.

Chris soon had a bag filled with Silva's clothes in one hand and Silva's hand in the other as they left the store, traveling through the still crowded mall. It actually looked more crowded now than it had before. When he checked a nearby clock stationed on the wall, he saw that it was past noon.

Grrrgglee!

He blinked when a rumbling noise echoed out beside him, turned his head, and looked at Silva as she stared at her stomach, her cheeks flushed a light shade of red.

"Let's get something to eat before we continue shopping," he suggested.

"What is there to eat?" asked Silva.

"Lots of stuff. This mall has a food court. Let's go there, and you can choose to eat wherever you want."

"R-really?"

"Really."

Silva seemed startled that he was letting her choose at first, but then her eyes brightened as she nodded with enthusiasm.

The food court was just a massive outdoor eating area. The Chula Vista Center was an outdoor mall. This particular area was a large and open space with hundreds of tables set up. Each table could seat about four people. Meanwhile, enclosing the space around the food court were the numerous fast-food chains that sold everything from Mexican food to Asian cuisine.

Silva looked overwhelmed by the sheer number of places to eat, turning her head this way and that as if she couldn't figure out where to look first. He let her adjust to the sudden change before asking where she wanted to eat.

"Um…" Silva's fangs poked out of her mouth as she bit her lip. Then she pointed at something. "I want to eat there. Is that okay?"

The place she had chosen to eat was called Fish Fillet, which made it very obvious what they sold. Several people sitting around outside were eating fish dishes like beer-battered fish sticks and the more healthy salmon salad.

"Yeah. We can eat there."

"Thank you."

Chris didn't know what she was thanking him for, but he shrugged and walked into the store with her. The moment they entered, Silva sniffed several times, her tail languidly swishing behind her.

He led the excited catgirl to the register and had her order something for herself. She ordered the lemon salmon salad, while he ordered fried shrimp. He also asked for two cups for water. The young man ringing up their order nodded and said their order would be right up as Chris paid for it.

After filling their cups with water, they found a seat inside. Silva took a sip of her water, but then drank deeply when she realized how parched she was. They had been moving around a lot. It was also unlikely that she'd had much water to drink since escaping from her abuser. Chris refilled her drink several times before she was satisfied.

"Order number 363! You're up!" someone called out and set a tray on the counter.

"That's us," Chris said.

He stood up and went over to grab the tray, returning to the table where he set the tray down and handed Silva her salmon salad. The girl looked like she was about to eat with her hands. However, Chris handed her a fork, which she awkwardly held and used to eat with. Meanwhile, since he was eating beer-battered shrimp, he used his hands.

As he ate, he noticed Silva staring at his food. Giving her a somewhat forced smile, he grabbed one of the shrimp and held it out to her.

"Want a bite?" he asked.

"C-can I?" asked Silva.

He shrugged. "Go ahead."

"In that case…" Silva reached up and tucked a stray strand of silver hair behind her ear as she leaned over. It was a surprisingly mature action. She opened her cute little mouth, revealing sharp canines as she bit down on the shrimp with a crunch. Silva leaned back and blinked several times as she chewed the shrimp. "It's very crunchy… but kinda oily."

"It is fried." Chris popped another piece of shrimp into his mouth and chewed. "Fried food is always oily."

"Grams would never let me try fried food," Silva admitted. "She said it was bad for me. And my previous guardian… well…"

"He barely let you eat at all, right?" Chris asked. Silva nodded. "Well, with me, you will be able to eat as much as you want."

His words caused her to break out into a smile.

They shopped for several more hours after finishing lunch. Chris needed to make a stop at a local catgirl store, where he bought dietary supplements. The supplements he bought were the Pedigree brand, which were known for producing some of the best catgirl products around. He also secretly slipped in a few toys for catgirls.

Once all their shopping was done, they hopped onto a bus that would take them back home. Silva must have been exhausted because she fell asleep against him the moment they sat down. He let the catgirl rest. When they reached their stop, he lifted her into his arms and carried her to his apartment.

"Hey, if it isn't Chris!" someone greeted him as he entered the lobby. It was a young man with wavy blond hair and blue eyes. He was wearing a sweater and jeans. With his masculine features, he looked like a model.

"Alex," Chris greeted as Silva shifted in his arms, rubbing her cheek against his shoulder. The catgirl in his arms did not go unnoticed by Alex.

"I'd heard you had gotten yourself a catgirl," Alex said with a grin. "I didn't realize she'd be so young, though. I figured you were more into the buxom type. So little kids do it for you?"

"If you said that as a joke, I feel like I should tell you it's not very funny." Chris would have shrugged, but he didn't want to wake the girl in his arms. "I actually discovered Silva and am taking care of her for the time being. That's all."

"I know." Alex chuckled. "I heard the police came by this morning. Seeing the catgirl in your arms, it's easy enough to figure out what's going on. Anyway, I'm heading to my job. See you later."

"Yeah. See you."

As Alex walked out the door he just entered from, Chris headed toward the elevator, went up to the second floor, and traveled to his room. Silva was still sleeping. He went into his bedroom and set her on the bed, then traveled back into the living room. Chris checked his phone. It was 3:30pm now, too late to head over to the Kickboxing Center like he'd promised Captain Tanner. He also didn't think he could leave Silva alone in the apartment yet. He needed to be there in case of a panic attack.

He scrolled through his contact list and selected Captain Tanner's caller ID, then placed the phone against his ear and waited for someone to pick up. It looked like he'd be missing his daily exercise on top of school today.

chapter 5

The next morning, Chris woke up with his head on his desk. He groaned as he sat up, feeling the slight crick in his neck, and stretched his arms above his head. His back popped several times as a dull ache permeated his back, neck, and shoulders. Wow. This did not feel pleasant at all.

As he tried to rid himself of the stiffness in his shoulders and spine, he glanced at the computer in front of him. The monitor was still on, showing what he'd been working on last night: A drawing of a beautiful girl created with an anime style of artwork. The girl was a redhead with fox ears, two tails, and large breasts. His drawing was nearly complete. He just needed to add a few small details to her clothing. The fact that it wasn't finished meant he must have fallen asleep while he was working.

He grabbed the stylus sitting on the desk off to his left. Next he pulled his waicom tablet over. His tablet wasn't the best. It was a 15.6 inch Cintiq 16 and featured a 1920x1080 HD display, which was decent but not as good as some of the other tablets like the Cintiq Pro 24. However, Chris was not a professional artist so he had no real need for a more expensive tablet.

Chris finished up his commission, saved the file as a PSD and a JPG, and then opened his email. He quickly found the commissioner's email address. Attaching the two files as a compressed folder, he typed out a quick message and clicked the send button.

Yawning as the email sent, Chris waited for a little bit before closing down all of his programs and shutting off his computer. It was a custom made computer that a friend had created for him. He didn't know exactly what kind of computer it was, but it featured a mostly black casing with red lights on the front, while the left side had a glass casing that let him see all the components inside. It looked cool. That said, all he really needed to know about this computer was that it was stupidly powerful.

Chris stood up and began getting a start on his day. He grabbed his clothes, took a shower, and got dressed, then made breakfast for himself and his new roommate.

He decided to make a Greek yogurt parfait this morning, which he created by spooning Greek yogurt into two bowls, adding honey, and mixing in crushed granola, slices of strawberries, some blueberries, and blackberries. He also mixed the dietary supplement into Silva's portion. It looked like a protein powder. After placing the bowls on the table with some spoons, he went back into his bedroom.

Silva was still asleep. She was lying on her side and huddled underneath the blanket, her small mouth open as she breathed through it. Soft whistling sounds emitted from her mouth as the ears on her head twitched of their own accord.

How long had it been since he'd had someone aside from himself in his bed? Not since his girlfriend of last year broke up with him. He remembered how she'd come over to his place, wear his T-shirts as pajamas, and sleep with him like this. Of course, back then, he would be in bed with her, but seeing this cute sleeping catgirl still gave him a nostalgic feel.

He found himself loathe to wake her up when she was sleeping so peacefully. Actually, Chris found that he wanted to watch her for a bit longer, but he reached out and gently brushed some hair from her face before shaking her awake.

"Mreow?" Silva sat up in bed and rubbed her eyes with the back of her hand. Her long tail came out from beneath the covers and waved languidly back and forth with a hypnotic sway. "Is it morning… alreaaady?"

As girl yawned, she stretched her arms above her head, causing the large T-shirt she wore to become rumpled and creased.

"Yeah. It's morning. I've got breakfast ready too, so come on and head to the dinner table."

"Mrrr… okay."

Chris almost laughed when he saw how the catgirl still wasn't making any attempt at moving. He took her by the hands and guided her off the bed, then walked backwards as he led her into the living room.

Breakfast was eaten mostly in silence. Silva still wasn't fully awake. She scooped up the parfait mechanically and stuck the spoon into her mouth, but she missed several times and got it on her face, prompting Chris to grab a napkin so he could wipe it off. The only noise in the living room was the TV, which he turned on so he could watch the news.

"… And in other news, police have recently discovered a catgirl slave trafficking operation based off the coast of San Diego, California," the newscaster was saying. Silva's ears twitched. "The police have reason to believe the Triad might be involved in this operation since a number of these catgirls seem to have been shipped to and from China, though no evidence of their involvement has come to light."

Chris kept one ear on the news, but most of his attention was focused on Silva, whose tail was flicking agitatedly. Even her ears looked like they were bristling a little.

"You okay?" he asked.

Silva looked startled when he suddenly spoke up, but then she calmed down and nodded. "I am okay. I was just… remembering my previous guardian."

"Because of the news?"

Silva nodded again. "He treated me and the other catgirls like slaves. He called us toys. He used to say since catgirls couldn't get by without humans, we were basically just toys for humans to play with."

Chris needed to take a deep breath to keep calm. "That man's views are ones I've heard expressed before. I'm still shocked people think like that." He looked past her and toward the television. He couldn't see the screen very well, but it looked like they had switched to reporting on the weather. "While it is true that catgirls have formed a strong relationship with humans, it isn't like all catgirls live with humans. There are some who live on their own, work for themselves, and don't necessarily live among humans. Really, the only thing a catgirl needs a human for is when it's mating season, and that's what breeders are for."

Silva didn't say anything, just nodded her head and continued eating. However, she kept looking at Chris as he polished off his Greek yogurt. He waited for her to finish, then took both their bowls to the kitchen, washed them out, and placed them in the dishwasher.

"I need to head over to school," Chris said at last. "Do you think you will be okay if I let you stay here by yourself?"

The moment Chris asked this, Silva paled, the blood draining from her face. She bit her lip. It looked like she was struggling as her face scrunched up, but then she took a deep breath and nodded.

"Yes. I'll be fine on my own."

Chris wasn't entirely convinced she'd be okay if he left her alone, but he really didn't have a choice. He'd called out yesterday because he needed to take Silva to the doctor for a checkup. However, he didn't have any reason to call out of school today, and saying he needed to stay here with Silva was not a good enough reason. That wouldn't fly with Professor Shinomiya.

Before he left, Chris showed Silva how to use the remote, teaching her how to access all of his programs like Netflix, Youtube, FUNImation, and HiDIVE. He also showed her the leftovers she could eat when she got hungry. He still had some salmon that he'd cooked for her the other day. Once he was sure Silva would be okay, Chris grabbed his backpack, said goodbye, and left.

Yet even as he made his way to the bus stop, a little bit of worry wriggled its way into his chest.

Would Silva really be okay on her own?

***

Chris arrived at class a little later than usual, which explained why quite a few of his peers had arrived before him. Most of them had broken into groups and were chatting amongst themselves, but a few also sat alone, reading a book or writing something in their notebooks. He found Anastasia Pierce sitting in the same chair she had the last time he saw her.

"Good morning," he greeted as he walked up to her and sat down.

"Good morning yourself," Anastasia said as she raised an eyebrow. Her lips curled into a wry smile. "You weren't here yesterday. Don't tell me you decided to ditch school? I thought you were a diligent student, unlike that slacker Professor Shinomiya kicked out of class."

There was a tone of teasing in her voice. Chris didn't take her words too seriously as he chuckled.

"I wasn't ditching." His chuckling vanished as he remembered why he hadn't gone to school yesterday. "An emergency situation came up, so I had to call out. I let Professor Shinomiya know I wouldn't be here in advance. Speaking of, would you mind if I copied down your notes from yesterday?"

"I suppose not, though in return, I want you to tell me why you weren't in class the other day." When Chris opened his mouth to respond, Anastasia shushed him by placing a finger to his lips. "You don't have to tell me right now. Focus on writing those notes. You can tell me what happened when you take me out to lunch after class ends."

Chris noticed how she said "when you take me out to lunch" as if him doing so was already a foregone conclusion. Of course, since she was lending him her notes in exchange, it basically was. He decided to just accept her advice with a nod and pulled out his notebook while Anastasia slid her laptop over to him. She had already opened the word document filled with her notes from the previous day.

It looked like their lesson the previous day had expanded upon catgirl reproduction. The notes referenced how catgirls are induced ovulators, meaning they don't ovulate unless they are bred. However, the notes also mention that it was very hard for catgirls to breed, though the notes had this added as an anecdote instead of an expanded explanation. It spoke more about the birthing process itself, stating that pregnancy for a catgirl lasted about 6 months, which was three to four months shorter than most human pregnancies.

Just as he finished taking the notes, the doors opened and Professor Shinomiya walked in. Chris slid the laptop back to Anastasia as the professor walked onto the lecture podium and set her water bottle and purse on the teacher's desk. The class went silent as she grabbed a remote from the desk and turned on the screen behind her.

"Yesterday, you all learned about catgirl pregnancy," Professor Shinomiya began, getting right into the lecture. "So today, we're going to be learning about why it's so hard for a catgirl to get pregnant in the first place. I only briefly explained this the other day, but I'll be going into a lot more details now."

As she spoke, she pressed another button on the remote, which pulled up a PowerPoint presentation. The presentation was titled *Genetic Incompatibility*. It had the image of a catgirl and a human male holding hands on one side. On the other side were a series of notes marked by bulletin points.

"The biggest reason catgirls have trouble getting pregnant is because there aren't that many humans who are genetically compatible with them," Professor Shinomiya explained. "In human relationships, genetic compatibility has more to do with partner preferences than actually being genetically compatible. The GenePartner project inspired by a famous study performed by Doctor Wedekind at the University of Bern in Switzerland led to the development of a formula that combines the diversity factor studied by Doctor Wedenkind, together with several other evolutionary factors researched and developed by the Swiss Institute for Behavioral Genetics."

Chris jotted down everything the professor said, though he didn't do so word for word since some of what she said wasn't necessarily important. He created bulletin points for keywords like Doctor Wedenkind, the GenePartner project, and the GenePartner formula, which could apparently make an accurate prediction of the strength for the basis of a long-lasting and fulfilling romantic relationship between individuals.

As he diligently wrote in his notebook, Chris wondered if this was the reason none of his relationships had worked out. In middle school, high school, and even college, Chris had been in quite a few relationships. All of them ended quite abruptly. His longest lasting relationship was with his last girlfriend, whom he dated for about six months before she broke up with him.

"Catgirl genetic compatibility is quite different from human genetic compatibility," Professor Shinomiya suddenly switched topics. "The GeneProject formula is meant to show whether or not a relationship will last. On the other hand, when a person refers to genetic compatibility between catgirls and humans, they are talking about how high a human male's chances are of helping a catgirl conceive a child."

Professor Shinomiya paused here to take a drink from her water bottle. This also gave the students time to write down what she said.

"While catgirls generally produce a litter of about three or four children per birth, catgirl birthrates are extremely low, which is why the human to catgirl population is about one catgirl for every twenty humans. This is because most humans do not have a high compatibility with catgirls. Generally speaking, the chances of a human male impregnating a catgirl are between 5 and 25%, a relatively low number. Among the human male population, only about .5% of them have a higher genetic compatibility rating with catgirls, and even then, the highest we've seen in recent studies among this .5% has been someone with a 50% genetic compatibility rate. That's still fairly low compared to human pregnancy."

As Professor Shinomiya went on to talk about the genetics involved, Chris thought about what these low birthrates meant for catgirls on a grander scale. He didn't like where his thoughts took him.

Part of him wondered if their low birthrates were the reason catgirls were such easy targets for sex trafficking. He imagined that people involved like the Triad were fond of how difficult it was for a catgirl to get pregnant because it meant they could get more use out of them. Chris closed his eyes as a pained grimace crossed his face. The thoughts churning through his head caused his stomach to twist into knots.

"You okay?" Anastasia asked in a whisper.

"Yeah," Chris whispered back as he opened his eyes. "I'm fine."

Anastasia did not look convinced, but she didn't say anything.

With a sigh, Chris focused on writing down everything Professor Shinomiya was saying.

****

When Chris first left, Silva felt nervous about being on her own. Ever since she'd first woken up in his apartment, Chris had been a constant presence. There was something about him that helped soothe her mind. Being near him gave her a sense of comfort and caused her chest to feel warm, like she was being wrapped up in a soft blanket. With him gone, it felt like that warm blanket had been snatched away.

However, that only lasted until she found something to watch.

She was watching a show called *After the Rain*. It was about a part-time worker who falls in love with her middle-aged boss.

As she sat there with her knees curled into her chest, Silva found that she didn't really understand the story all that well. The people were speaking in a different language, she couldn't read the subtitles fast enough to keep up with what was going on, and she didn't understand enough about human culture to really get the nuances of what was happening.

That said, the artwork was very pretty.

As she watched Akira try and confess to her manager, only for her manager to somehow misunderstand her confession as her liking him as a manager instead of as a person, Silva placed herself in this girl's shoes. Suddenly, she was imagining what would happen if she confessed to Chris.

Heat rose to her cheeks and she quickly shook her head. There was no way she could do that. Aside from the fact that she wasn't sure how she felt for Chris, there was also the fact that she was not the kind of person who could date someone like him. What had her previous guardian called her? Used goods? She remembered him screaming something like that when Kuro attacked him and told her to run.

Silva fell over onto her side, eyes still locked on the screen as the ending credits and theme song played. As she thought about her fellow catgirls, her stomach twisted into knots. Guilt gnawed at her insides as she thought of how no one except her seemed to escape.

She buried her face into her knees.

****

When the first half of classes ended for the day, Chris took Anastasia to a small restaurant located on school campus.

San Diego State University had several places to eat. The place they were eating at was called The Garden. It was a restaurant that allowed people to build their own salads.

Chris had gone with a salad made from kale, spinach, and romaine lettuce. He'd added grilled chicken and strawberries, then dressed it up with a citrus based salad dressing. As a side dish, he had a bowl of brown rice.

The citrus dressing complimented the strawberries and created a nice contrast with the chicken, which was lightly seasoned with salt and pepper to give it only a little taste. As he and Anastasia sat at a small table outside the restaurant, the girl, who was leafing through her own tofu salad, gave him an even gaze.

"Now you can tell me why you weren't in class the other day." She leaned forward as her eyes gleamed. "I'm curious to know what you were doing that was so important you had to skip out."

Chris sighed but realized he wasn't going to get out of this until he told her about what happened, so he started with how he had come across an unconscious catgirl on his way home from the kickboxing center. He talked about how she'd been injured, how she'd panicked when she'd woken up, how she had run away from her previous home, and even how the police had gotten involved.

There were some things he didn't tell her about. Chris had no intention of mentioning the more awkward moments like how he'd washed Silva in the bath or anything like that. Of course, he deemed those more intimate details unnecessary. This girl was just someone he sat next to in class. They weren't dating, so there was no need to inform her about anything.

When he finished, Anastasia leaned back and covered her hand with her mouth. She seemed shocked. Her eyes were wide as she stared at his face. When she finally pulled her hand from her mouth, her surprised demeanor changed back to a calm expression as she leaned forward.

"That's a pretty unbelievable story," she said. "The Catgirl Protection Bureau is pretty strict when it comes to handing out Catgirl Guardianship Licenses. It took me six tries before I was able to pass their exams. I just can't believe someone who would abuse catgirls like that was able to pass their exams so easily."

"It's not as if the exams are perfect." Chris shook his head as he speared a piece of chicken with his fork. "They use decently rigorous psychological tests and assessments to determine whether or not someone is mentally stable and nurturing enough to become the guardian of a catgirl. However, the tests themselves are still fairly standard. If someone knows enough about psychology, it's very easy to create a fake personality that bluffs the tests."

"But that can't be so easy, right?" asked Anastasia.

"It isn't easy, but it's not impossible either," Chris answered.

As he chewed on the chicken, Chris thought about who could have bluffed their way through such a test. It would have to be someone who had a high degree of knowledge in psychology. A therapist could easily bluff their way through a test like that, but so could a professional con artist who made a living off scamming people. There were some individuals living on the streets who had learned to read other people and act in a manner that would draw sympathy from that person. Whether or not Silva's abuser was someone like that, Chris couldn't say.

"In order to retain a Catgirl Guardianship License, a person has to take psychological examinations, tests, and assessments once a year. While the tests do change yearly, it isn't as if they change so much that you can't use your previous experiences to pass." Chris gazed at Anastasia as she finally began eating. "You haven't failed once since you passed the first evaluation, right?"

"Well, no..." Anastasia admitted as she chewed her salad.

"So there you have it." Chris shrugged. "Once someone passes the test, they can use their previous experience to pass every consecutive test. There are only so many methods people can use to evaluate someone."

"I guess..."

Silence reigned for awhile after they finished speaking so they could eat their food. Chris used that time to think about Silva. He hoped she was okay at home alone. To be perfectly honest, he didn't feel comfortable leaving the catgirl by herself yet. It would have been better if he could have stayed home for a few days and watched after her until she felt more comfortable in her new environment.

"What are you going to do now?" asked Anastasia after she finished eating.

"You mean about Silva?"

"Yes."

Chris leaned back in his seat and placed his hands on the table. In truth, he already knew what he was going to do.

"The Catgirl Protection Bureau has temporarily placed Silva in my custody until the current situation is resolved, so

I'll be watching after her for now. After that…" He took in a deep breath and sighed. "It will mostly depend on Silva, but once the matter regarding her previous guardian has been dealt with, I'll ask her if she wants to continue living with me. I have experience with looking after catgirls, so I'm confident in my ability to watch her."

"So you're going to let her stay with you?" Anastasia raised an eyebrow. "Won't that make it hard for you to have a relationship? I don't know about other girls, but if I was dating a man and found out he was living with a catgirl, I would break up with him."

"You'd break up with someone you love if he was living with a catgirl?" Chris asked.

"Of course I would," Anastasia said as if the reason should be obvious. However, when she saw the expression on Chris's face, she sighed and gave him an even expression. "Look, I don't think I need to tell you this, but catgirls are incredibly popular with men. Men love them. That's why becoming a breeder is such a popular career choice for young men between the ages of 18 and 25. Who wouldn't want to have sex with a willing young female that has cat ears and a tail? Catgirls are like the ultimate furry fetish."

"Well, I guess I can't argue with you there," Chris admitted with a sigh. "But what if your boyfriend isn't interested in catgirls? What if the catgirl in question is just a child he took in because she had nowhere to go?"

Anastasia grimaced. "I guess I could allow something like that... but it would really depend on the situation." Shaking her head, the woman's expression cleared as she gave him a firm look. "And you didn't answer my question."

Chris gave her a helpless smile and shrugged his shoulders. "I don't really have to worry about that. I haven't dated since my last girlfriend broke up with me several months ago, and somehow, I can't really see myself entering another relationship right now. I've already got my hands full with college, taking art commissions, my training at the kickboxing center, and now watching after Silva. My current lifestyle just doesn't allow me the time to develop a proper relationship with anyone."

"So I see." Anastasia frowned as if something was bothering her, but she didn't say anything regarding the matter. "Well, I guess that's just how it is."

Chris didn't know what she meant by that, and he wouldn't find out since their classes were starting again. After saying goodbye to Anastasia, he made his way toward his next class.

****

Aside from his catgirl related courses, Chris also took several prerequisite courses. His current core classes included Anatomy and Physiology, English Composition, Quantitative Analysis, Psychology, and Communication. He only took two general education classes each day. Monday and Fridays were his Anatomy and Physiology plus his English Composition classes, Tuesday and Thursday was Quantitative Analysis and Psychology, and Wednesday was Communication.

It was Wednesday, so aside from his Catgirl Biology Course, which he took three days a week, he was also taking Communication. It was a 4 hour long class that involved listening to a man called Professor Colbare lecture them on communication between races. The course was actually called Interracial Communication. It was primarily about communicating with people whose cultural background differed from your own. Chris was taking that class because he thought it would help him learn how to communicate better with catgirls.

After class ended, Chris traveled to the Kickboxing Center, where he spent an hour exercising and sparring with Tanner. The man had let him know that he'd been pretty disappointed when Chris called out the other day. However, he also understood the situation, which Chris had made sure to explain so the man knew exactly why he hadn't been able to come in.

By the time Chris arrived home, it was early evening, 4:30pm, and he was worried about Silva. He hoped she was okay. As he stepped out of the elevator and speed walked toward his door, he imagined coming home to find Silva having a panic attack.

"MREOW!!!!"

This worry went into overdrive when a familiar scream rang through the hallway. He broke into a run, nearly crashing into his door as he fumbled with his keys. Chris barely managed to unlock the door in his haste. He swung the door open and practically ran inside.

And then he paused.

He had expected many things when he returned home, but in all the horrible scenarios he imagined, a naked and soaking wet catgirl running around his living room was not it.

Slowly shutting the door, he called out to the girl as she leapt onto the couch, ran across its length, leapt off the couch, and somehow did a somersault in midair. It was impressive, especially since her eyes were closed.

"Silva, are you okay?" asked Chris.

"C-Chris!" Silva ran over to him, and Chris was surprised when the girl nearly bowled him over. He took a step back to steady himself as his front became soaking wet. Meanwhile, Silva was blinking rapidly as she stared at him, her eyes bloodshot. "I-I got soap in my eyes and it really hurts! W-what should I do?!"

As the water from Silva's body soaked into his clothes, Chris registered her words and snorted to contain his laughter.

All that worry for nothing.

chapter 6

"I hope all of you studied because your test on catgirl pregnancy is today," Professor Shinomiya said as she stood on the podium.

Her words caused a chorus of groans from the students. Chris didn't join them, but even Anastasia looked put out by the idea of taking a test. Even though he didn't join in, he did understand how everyone else felt. Tests were and probably always would be the bane of every student's existence.

"Stop complaining," Professor Shinomiya scolded them. "Your test is to write a two-page essay on catgirl childbirth and how certified Catgirls Doctors help them give birth safely. You have until class ends to finish this. Let me also remind you that all essays must be handwritten." She glanced at Anastasia and her laptop. "No computers."

Anastasia frowned at the professor, but then slowly put her laptop away, pulled out a notebook and a pencil, and opened it to an empty page. There was a look of distaste on her face. Chris only studied her for a second before turning his attention back to his own paper.

"Is everyone ready?" asked Professor Shinomiya. No one said anything. "In that case, you may begin."

As the sound of pencils scratching against paper echoed around the lecture hall, Chris studied the blank page for several seconds, thinking about his answer, before putting pencil to paper and beginning to write.

Catgirl pregnancy was always something of a delicate issue. It didn't happen often, but when it did happen, at the very least three catgirls would be born. This was regardless of the size or breed of the catgirl in question. Even a Munchkin catgirl would give birth to at least that many catgirls, which often caused issues during pregnancy.

Actually, back before safe birthing practices were put into place, it wasn't all that unusual for catgirls to die from pregnancy. The shock of birthing so many children put a huge strain on the catgirl's body. This was especially true for smaller breeds of catgirl. Some catgirls like the Munchkin catgirl had a harder time giving birth because of their size.

That said, it wasn't as big of an issue with larger breeds like Maine Coons, Savanah, and Siberian catgirls.

In most cases, catgirl births were very similar to human births. However, a greater emphasis was placed on monitoring the catgirl while she was giving birth. Standard practices involved one nurse monitoring the catgirl's health constantly, while the other helped deliver the babies. A certified Catgirl Doctor was also required to be in attendance in case something happened. If the there was a spike in the catgirl's vitals, depending on the situation, the Catgirl Doctor would need to perform a C-section.

Even before the birthing, it was important for catgirls to be monitored and receive regular checkups during their pregnancy. With human women, check-ups would happen once each month for weeks four through twenty-eight. However, for a catgirl, it was generally once each week from the moment it becomes known they are pregnant until the actual due date.

It took Chris a little more than half the allotted time to finish his essay. When he was done, he stood up and made his way down the stairs under the watchful eyes of everyone who hadn't finished. Some of them looked a little shocked, others resigned, and a few were even glaring at him. He didn't quite understand that. However, he tried not to let their actions bother him as he went over to Profess Shinomiya and handed in his paper.

"I see you're done early again." Professor Shinomiya grabbed his paper before he could set it on her desk and read through it. Chris didn't say anything as the woman narrowed her eyes, frowned, then sighed and set his paper on her desk. "Your essay is succinct and well-written as always."

Chris shrugged. "I just wrote it using your notes."

"Hmph. It takes more than memorizing notes in class to get good grades." Professor Shinomiya seemed to be hinting at something regarding his dedication to his catgirl studies, but Chris didn't care to think on that too hard. His professor apparently didn't either since she changed the subject. "How is the catgirl situation?"

"It's going well so far," Chris answered. "Silva has adapted to her new living situation pretty well. She's also not having any nightmares or other issues like I was afraid would happen."

"Other issues?" asked Professor Shinomiya.

"She is living with a man." Chris shrugged. "Considering what happened to her when she was living with her previous guardian, I wouldn't have been surprised if she feared all men, but she hasn't given me any indication of that she's bothered by me."

Actually, while Silva wasn't what he would call clingy, she did seem more affectionate than he would have expected. Chris didn't know any rape victims outside of her, so he didn't know how they reacted to members of the same sex as their abuser, but he always pictured them as being afraid of men. Maybe that was just because he probably wouldn't like men if that situation happened to him.

Silva was nothing like that. After her first few days of living with him, she had begun sitting much closer to him on the couch, close enough that their thighs would touch. She never leaned against him, but it wasn't unusual for her to fall asleep. During those times she would lay with her head on his lap. He didn't know if she was aware of it, but whenever she fell asleep, he would stroke her hair. It was surprisingly therapeutic.

"It's good that she is adjusting well, but you should also remain vigilant." Professor Shinomiya paused here for emphasis, or maybe dramatic effect. Chris almost gulped when she frowned at him. "Even if she doesn't seem to be exhibiting any signs of distress, there may be some underlying side effects that don't become readily apparent until later. Be sure to keep looking after her."

"You don't have to tell me that," Chris said with a frown.

"I'm just making sure you understand," Professor Shinomiya said before waving her hand through the air.

"Anyway, since you finished the essay, you are free to leave if you want."

Chris pondered leaving as he looked around the lecture hall. All the other students were diligently writing their essays. He glanced at Anastasia, who looked like she was quietly cursing as she erased something. She didn't look too pleased. Then again, unlike everyone else, she had a heavy preference toward using her laptop. He wondered how long it had been since she used pencil and paper to write anything.

"I'll be heading out then," Chris said, waving goodbye to his teacher.

He left the lecture hall, wandered through the building, and exited seconds later. The bright sun hit his eyes, causing him to squint. Despite the sun being incredibly bright that day, without a cloud in the sky to block it, the air was still chilly.

It was still really early in the afternoon, so he couldn't even go out to get lunch yet. That being the case, Chris decided to take a walk around the college campus, which was fairly large. It spanned 283 acres worth of land. Something like that. It was also quite beautiful. There were several parks located around the campus where students could sit. These parks were filled with green grass, large oak trees, and tables for people to sit around.

As he walked through some of these parks, he saw other students sitting around, talking, laughing, or sitting alone as they read a book. One of them, a catgirl with hair that reminded him of a cheetah, was sleeping with her belly up in the sun. Chris shook his head and continued walking... then he paused when he caught sight of something.

A brawl was happening several yards out. It looked like a group of students were picking on one of the other students. He didn't recognize the ones attacking, but he did know the one being attacked, or at least knew his name. His slick-backed hair, vicious eyes, and rumpled clothing gave him away.

It was Jason Barker.

Chris still remembered how the man had gotten kicked out of Professor Shinomiya's class several days ago because of his crass comments. It was coincidentally the same day he found Silva lying underneath that bridge in Memorial Park near his apartment complex.

He was about to leave since this fight didn't involve him, but then he noticed something. Hiding behind Jason, pressed against his back, was a shivering girl with pointed triangle-shaped ears covered in orange fur and a cat tail of the same color sticking out of her back.

It was hard for him to believe his eyes. In fact, Chris rubbed his eyes several times to make sure he wasn't seeing things, but no matter how many times he looked, it really did look like Jason was protecting a catgirl from those men surrounding them. That was seriously not something he would have ever expected this man to do.

With a sigh, he made his way over to where the group was. If it had just been Jason, he wouldn't have bothered getting himself involved, but, well, he couldn't not get involved when there was a catgirl in need of help. If he had to say what his weakness was, then they would be his one true weakness.

As he walked over to them, Chris caught what sounded like the tail end of their conversation.

"What the fuck, man?! You don't have to be a fucking bastard! All we were trying to do was talk to her!" one of the men shouted. He looked like a pretty typical jock. His well-defined body was covered in muscles barely concealed by his tight shirt and jeans. He was also wearing a sports jacket with the logo for the San Diego State University's basketball team, the Aztecs.

Jason rolled his eyes as he spat on the grass. "You say you were just talking to her, but I'm pretty sure grabbing a girl hard enough to leave a bruise and making her cry isn't 'just talking,' douchewad."

"Don't be such a fucking pussy, man," another one said. He was larger than the jock, but his size came from his fat, not his muscle. "We only wanted to see if she'd like to come bowling with us. What are you? Some kind of social justice warrior? Pfft!"

It looked like there were four of them. Two of them were the jock and the fat man. Well, they were all wearing sports jackets, so Chris felt it was reasonable to assume they were on the sports team as well. As the fat guy made a joke about Jason being a social justice warrior, which Chris found funny for the opposite reason these people did, the others laughed.

Jason didn't take well to that.

With a vein bulging on his forehead, the man dashed forward and threw his full weight into a punch that slammed into the fat guy's face. It must have been a heavy punch. Even from a distance, Chris saw the way the guy's cheek wobbled when it was struck. He also went down like a sack of bricks, landing on his rear end and holding a hand to his face as he looked up at Jason in shock.

"What the fuck?! You actually hit me!"

"Thank you, Captain Obvious!" Jason snapped. "I didn't know that! I appreciate you telling me what I did to you!"

"That does it!" The jock's face darkened. "Let's teach this loser a lesson!"

The jock and his two friends quickly moved in for the kill, which caused the catgirl hiding behind Jason to squawk in fright. Jason's eyes narrowed as he adopted a really sloppy fighting stance. It was clear that despite his punch being quite powerful, he had no actual combat training. Even an untrained eye could probably recognize that.

Chris decided to attack before they could close the distance. He didn't care about Jason. However, he didn't want the catgirl accidentally getting hurt by this brawl.

Since it looked like the jock was already too close to Jason for Chris to intercept, he raced in front of the other two. They both stopped, skidding along the ground, their faces expressing surprise. Chris used that momentary surprise to his advantage.

He took two steps forward, moving into the left one's range, then launched a low kick. His attack caught the man in the leg at the joint between his thigh and calf. This forced him onto a knee, which lowered his head, and Chris had no qualms about kicking a man while he was down like this. He hopped onto his left foot, raised his leg, rotated his body, and threw a side kick that caught the man right in the face.

Blood spurted from the man's nose as he fell backward. He hit the ground with a thud and didn't get back up.

"What the hell?! Who the hell are you?!" asked the other one.

"Are you really asking someone who just knocked your friend out cold who he is?" Chris asked, feeling a little incredulous.

"Shut up! Are you another Social Justice Warrior?! Fuck you, you goddamn SJW pansy!"

The man rushed him, but Chris remained confident as he adopted a southpaw kickboxing stance, right hand and right foot forward. He wasn't left-handed. However, he found that most people had more trouble dealing with a southpaw stance than they did an orthodox stance.

As the man came in with a straight punch that had no real coordination behind it, Chris stepped to his right, raised his hand, and blocked the attack with his forearm. A dull thud echoed through the grassy field. He pushed the man's arm away from him, leaving the man open to retaliation.

His first punch, a straight jab with his right hand, knocked the man's head back. The man blinked several times as if dazed. He shook his head once, then came back at Chris again. He swung several times, but all of his attacks were wide hooks that even an infant could have dodged. Chris almost wanted to lecture the man on his sloppy punches. Despite his lack of talent or skill, he clearly had some strength to him since Chris could feel the shifts in the wind as the man threw his attacks.

"Quit. Dodging!" The man shouted in anger.

"Well, if that's what you want," Chris said.

He stopped dodging the man's attacks and stood still, but that didn't mean he planned on taking the hit. Raising his right hand, he blocked the man's wide punch, took a single step forward, and threw his left hand in a proper hook that connected solidly with the man's face. There was a satisfying crack that echoed from the impact as the man spun around. Despite the hit being quite solid, Chris's opponent was still standing, though from the way his knees wobbled, it was clear that punch had rattled his brain.

Chris decided to finish it.

He took another two steps forward, hit the man with a jab of his right hand, then came in and decked him with another left hook. Regardless of how durable this guy was, very few people could stand after having their brain so thoroughly rattled. This guy was no different. He fell to the ground, still conscious, but obviously unable to get up. He probably wouldn't be able to move for awhile.

With the two on his end taken care of, Chris turned around to watch Jason deal with the last one.

He wondered if the sweat rolling down his face was real or imagined.

Chris understood that very few people actually had real combat training, that it was rare for anyone to know how to throw a proper punch. He remembered watching fights in his high school and thinking about how he never wanted to be one of those people who were forced to resort to grapples and overpowering someone with their weight to win a fight. Of course, Chris had never been a tall guy. At 5'10", he was considered slightly above average in height.

In either event, while he understood that very few people knew how to fight, seeing two people who clearly had no combat experience or training duking it out made him wonder if slamming his face into a tree would help him forget the sight.

Jason and the jock were throwing sloppy, half-hazard punches at each other. They didn't try to dodge or block. One would punch. The other would take the hit. Then the other would punch, while the previous puncher took the hit. It was like they were having a contest over who could take more punches.

Was this what some women meant when they talked about male pissing contests?

Chris wondered if he should intervene, but just as the thought crossed his mind, Jason threw a punch that landed squarely on the jock's nose. A loud *crunch* echoed through the clearing. The man dropped like a sack of potatoes. While it had taken a lot longer to deal with this guy than Chris believed it should have, that last hit had been pretty solid.

With his battle over, Jason stood straighter and looked around. There was blood dripping from his mouth where he'd split his lip, the area under his left eye was red, and he had a black right eye that looked like it was about to begin swelling.

However, he didn't seem to notice his own injuries as he glanced at Chris.

"You're… from that fucking professor's class, aren't you?" he asked, having recognized Chris.

"I'm surprised you recognize me since we never spoke in class," Chris said.

"Che." Jason spat on the grass. "It's hard not to recognize people who are in that bitch's class."

Chris really had to wonder about this guy. He seemed like such a bad person. He was crude, said rude things about catgirls and professions related to them, and called the professors at this school crass names, and yet he protected a catgirl from some men who looked like they had been harassing her. At least, that was what Chris assumed had happened.

"Um, excuse me?" The catgirl in question suddenly spoke up. Chris and Jason turned to face her.

Now that he was getting a better look at her, Chris could see that she was quite cute. She wasn't very tall, reaching to about his chest, but she had surprisingly large breasts. He didn't know how big they were. However, the shirt she was wearing clearly wasn't suit for her body type. It stretched across her bust and lifted up, revealing her flat stomach. He assumed she was wearing a bra underneath since there was no way her boobs could naturally have that kind of lift without them, especially given their size, but he was beginning to understand why those jocks currently laid out on the grass had tried to pick her up.

Dudes like that would do anything to see those tits.

"What is it?" Jason grunted.

The catgirl flinched, perhaps at his tone or the expression on his face, but she pressed on anyway, giving him an earnest look.

"T-thank you for stepping in and protecting me from those men. I tried to tell them I wasn't interested, but they were being really persistent and wouldn't leave me alone. It was really frightening when they grabbed me."

"Whatever." Although Jason's single word answer seemed rude, when Chris looked his way, he saw the blush staining the other man's cheeks. Now that was startling. "Anyway, you should be more careful. Where is your next class?"

"Um… my next class is Human Bio-Cultural Origin with Professor Kobari," the catgirl said.

"Then let's go. Where's your stuff?"

"Huh? Oh, it's right here—wait! What are you doing?!"

Chris watched, flabbergasted, as Jason grabbed the girl's book bag and began walking in what he guessed was the direction of the catgirl's classroom. The girl chased after him, screaming about how she could carry her bag herself and that he didn't have to go so far. He could only shake his head.

"I don't believe it," he muttered. "Jason Barker is a tsundere."

He'd never met a real life tsundere before. The only time he'd seen anyone who matched that archetype was in anime… and normally, the tsundere was a cute Lolita girl. A male tsundere who was a delinquent was a new one to Chris.

Glancing at his phone, Chris noticed that it was nearly time for lunch. With one last look at the four men, two of which were just dazed and two who were unconscious, Chris began making his way toward the nearest restaurant. All this combat had made him hungry.

***

After school, Chris headed for the kickboxing center. He got dressed in his kickboxing clothes, simple workout shorts and a muscle shirt, and headed for the main area. Tanner was already there. It looked like the man was working with someone else at the moment, so Chris headed toward the stretching mat and began to limber up.

His stretches were all pretty basic stuff, but stretching was important. Exercising without stretching could result in injury.

He stood with his feet spread to create an isosceles triangle with the floor, bent over, and touched his left foot with his hands, then moved and touched his right foot. A slow burning sensation appeared in his lower back and legs. His calves also felt like they were a little stiff, so he used a roller to work out the knots in them before pressing his hands against the nearest wall and stretching his calves.

"You look like you're ready to spar."

Chris looked up when someone spoke to him and found Tanner standing several feet away, arms crossed and a grin on his face.

"I'm always ready to spar," Chris tossed that quip toward the man.

"Ha! Then get in the ring already! I was looking for a good punching bag!"

Despite the man's words, Tanner didn't actually use him as a punching bag. Their spars always consisted of the two trading attack and defense. Of course, Chris often had a harder time defending against Tanner than his trainer did him, but the guy was a veteran currently on the reserves list, so he didn't think it was fair to compare them. This man had way more experience in live combat than he did.

By the time their spar was done, Chris was breathing heavily as he drank some Gatorade to replenish the nutrients he lost while sweating. His body felt like it had been pounded with a mallet. He imagined the beef he sometimes saw hanging from butcher shops felt like this after they had been tenderized.

"Hey, Chris," Tanner suddenly said.

"What's up, Captain?"

"My catpanion wanted to know if you and your new housemate wanted to have dinner with us tonight," Tanner said. When Chris eyed him, the man scratched his cheek with a big finger. "I may have mentioned Silva to her, and she expressed an interest in meeting the girl."

Chris thought about it for a moment as he leaned against the ropes of the sparring ring, then shrugged.

"Well, I don't see why not, but I'll have to run it by Silva and see if she's okay with the idea."

Tanner gave Chris a smile that he couldn't place, like he knew something that Chris didn't, which honestly kind of bothered him. Sadly, before he could ask about that strange smile, Tanner spoke up.

"Just send me a text message if you decide to show up."

"Will do."

Since Chris didn't have much left to do there, he headed for the showers, changed into his regular clothes, and left the kickboxing center.

****

"Dinner with your gym coach?" Silva looked at him with a curious tilt of her head.

"I know it sounds a bit odd, but his catpanion said she wants to meet you. Apparently, Tanner told her about how I was living with you and expressed an interest in seeing you."

Chris and Silva were sitting on the couch as usual. The television was on, but they weren't really paying attention to what they were watching at the moment. Out of the corner of his eye, Chris saw the show that was playing, a cooking channel of some kind. It looked like the chef, a lady with blond hair who was on the beefy side, was cooking some kind of meat pie.

When Silva bit her lip, Chris added, "We don't have to go if you're uncomfortable with the idea."

"I don't really mind," Silva said, though Chris was certain she did mind and was saying this because she thought she needed to be polite.

"Are you sure?" Chris asked for confirmation. "I'm serious when I say we don't have to go. If you aren't comfortable being out of the house yet, I can just send Tanner a message saying we can't make it."

Silva wiggled her nose, which Chris thought was a cute gesture. He imagined what she'd look like if she had whiskers on her cheeks.

"I think… we should go," Silva said.

Chris wanted to ask if she was sure again, but since she had already said they should go twice, he sent Tanner a text message letting them know they would come by. He received a reply back saying dinner would be ready in about an hour and they should hop on over. Since they were both already dressed, it was a simple matter to hop onto a bus that would take them to their destination.

Tanner lived fifteen minutes from the kickboxing center, in a cul-de-sac next to Independence Park.

All the houses looked very similar to each other. Most of them were one story houses, but there were also a few two-story houses. They possessed shingled roofs of varying colors. Red. Tan. Orange. None of the houses seemed too drastically different from any other houses. As Chris and Silva hopped off the bus, they glanced around at the housing units with their picket fences, small gardens, and two-car driveways.

"These are nice houses," Silva murmured as she clung to his arm. She was shaking, but tried to ignore her own fear. "They remind me of the house I lived in with Grams."

"She lived in a cul-de-sac like this?" Chris asked. Silva nodded. "She must have had a lot of money. Most of these houses cost around a million dollars."

California was an expensive state to live in. While Chula Vista didn't have the same high cost as San Francisco or the San Diego Bay Area, it still cost about twice as much to live here as it did in other states like Arizona, Texas, or Oklahoma.

"I don't know how much that is," Silva admitted. "Is it a lot?"

"It's more than most people make in several decades," Chris said.

"Oh…" Silva paused. "Does that mean you don't make enough to live in a house like these ones?"

"Maybe when I graduate from college, I'll begin earning enough to live in an actual house like this, but not right now."

Chris and Silva began walking. There were several other people present as they made their way through the cul-de-sac, kids playing in the street or riding their bikes, adults walking their dogs, and couples out for a stroll. A few of those people greeted him and Silva, others stared, and some pointed at Silva and mentioned her cat ears and tail. As this happened, Silva's grip on his arm increased to the point where it kind of hurt.

"Are you sure you're okay?" asked Chris. Silva nodded, but she didn't speak, which caused him to sigh and wonder if she was really all right.

Tanner's house was the last building in a dead end. It was only one-story, had a two-car garage, and a red shingled roof. There was a massive oak tree in the front, which Silva looked at like she wanted to climb it. Chris had to tug on her hand to get her to keep moving. They made their way up to the front door, rang the doorbell, and waited.

"Hold on a sec!" a shout came from the other side. Silva flinched.

Loud thumping came seconds later, and the door suddenly opened to reveal a big man with dark skin standing in the entrance. He wore basic black slacks, a plain white shirt, and socks but no shoes. Silva shrank back and hid behind Chris. If the man noticed her reaction to his intimidating presence, he didn't let it show on his face as he smiled at them.

"Chris, good to see you," Tanner said. "And this must be your roommate. It's nice to finally meet you." When Silva continued to hide behind Chris, Tanner chuckled. "It looks like she's not fond of me."

"That's… not it," Silva said softly.

"She just hasn't been outside often since she started living with me," Chris said. "I'm sure meeting new people has made her nervous."

Chris still wasn't sure he understood why she wanted to leave the apartment when she clearly wasn't comfortable with the idea of meeting new people. It felt a lot like she was forcing herself to do something she didn't want. That said, he hadn't questioned her decision because he thought going outside was a good thing. She couldn't remain cooped indoors all day.

"It's fine," Tanner said with a wave of his hand. "Anyway, come on in. My catpanion is about finished with dinner."

Tanner led Chris and Silva inside. His house looked pretty typical, with carpet covering most of the floors except the hallway, which was tiled. There were various photos around the house, some hanging from the walls and some sitting on counters and tables. Most of them were of Tanner and a porcelain-skinned woman with dark hair, dark eyes, and black cat ears.

"Come on and sit in the living room," Tanner said as he led them into a living room that was about two times larger than the one in Chris's apartment. "Make yourselves at home. I'm just going to get Akari."

Chris did as suggested and sat down. Silva sat beside him, practically plastering herself against his torso. She was shivering. While he honestly didn't mind if she got close like this, her reaction really did concern him.

"If you're so nervous about meeting new people, why did you agree to come over here for dinner?" he asked.

"B-because this Tanner person is your friend, right?" said Silva. "If he's your friend, then I… shouldn't I meet him?"

"I'm not sure I understand your logic," Chris admitted. "We could always wait until you're more comfortable being outside before meeting new people."

But his words caused Silva to shake her head. "If I stay indoors like I have been… I'm afraid I'll grow so comfortable that I'd never leave. "Chris opened his mouth, but Silva continued in a much softer voice. "You've been very kind to me, but I think because of your kindness, I've been worried that I'm taking advantage of you. Grams always said I should repay my debts, but I haven't done anything to repay my debt to you."

"Why do you think you owe me a debt?" asked Chris. When Silva looked at him with big, wide eyes, he ran a hand through his hair. "I never helped you so you would owe me something, you know. I helped you because I was there and you needed help. That's it. I didn't do it expecting or even wanting to be repaid." He reached out to rub her head, paused when she flinched, and then placed his hand on her head and rubbed her hair. "You shouldn't feel any need to repay me."

"I… I'm not sure I feel the same way…"

Chris didn't know what else he could say to make this girl understand how he felt, and he wouldn't get the chance to right now since Tanner came in with a beautiful catgirl at his side. It was the woman from the pictures. He didn't know how old she was, but she looked young, with perfectly glossy and straight black hair, dark eyes, and youthful features. He would have said she was in her late teens or early twenties. Catgirls always looked young, but this woman, who had a definite Asian heritage, appeared even younger than most of the catgirls he knew.

Her eyes lit up as she saw them.

"It's really good to see you again, Chris. I didn't realize this girl was your catpanion." She had a very slight accent as she spoke, glancing at her partner with an exasperated gaze. "Tanner neglected to mention that to me."

Tanner rubbed the back of his head. "I didn't think she was."

"She's not," said Chris with a shake of his head as he stood up. Silva also stood up, looking both curious and wary of this new catgirl, though she seemed a little less frightened now than she had before.

"Really? Given how close you two were sitting, I would have expected… but maybe she's just using you as Tanner repellent," the catgirl said.

"I'm not sure how I feel about that," Tanner admitted.

"Silva, this is Akari," Chris said with a gesture toward the Asian catgirl. "She's Tanner's catpanion. They met when he was stationed at the US Military Base in Japan. Um, where was it again?"

"Okinawa," Tanner said.

"Right. Okinawa." Chris nodded.

"Um… it's nice to meet you," Silva said. She stepped forward, hesitated, then clasped her hands together and gave the other catgirl a short bow.

"You're awfully polite." Akari smiled and bowed as well, though her actions were far more refined. There was an elegance about this woman that few could match. He wondered if it was because of her Japanese heritage. "And please don't be afraid of Tanner. He might look big and scary, but he's actually really sweet and gentle."

"Again. I'm not sure how I feel about you saying that," Tanner said, but Akari just smiled at him.

After introductions were made, Akari directed them all into the kitchen, where they sat down as she got out the food. The scent of chicken casserole soon filled the air. Chris could almost feel his stomach gurgling as he watched her bring it over. Meanwhile, Silva looked like she was ten seconds away from drooling.

Dinner was prepared after they said a short prayer. Chris wasn't religious, and it didn't seem like Silva was either, but both of them prayed alongside Akari and Tanner anyway.

While everyone was eating, Akari did her best to engage Silva in conversation, and getting the silver-haired catgirl to say more than a few words at a time was like trying to pull out a cat's toenails. Silva wasn't really the most talkative individual. While she did speak with Chris whenever he was home, there were also long stretches of silence at his apartment when they were together. That said, she did talk more to him than she did Akari.

However, Akari was nothing if not persistent. She kept asking Silva questions that forced her to give more than single sentence answers. This had the effect of eventually getting Silva to talk more. By the time dinner was finished, his roommate was not only answering Akari's questions but also asking some of her own.

"By the way, what is a catpanion?" asked Silva. "You've all mentioned it several times before, but I've never heard of that until now."

Akari glanced at Chris, who looked away, then at Tanner, who just shrugged. She gave them both an annoyed look, as if lamenting how unhelpful they were. Then she turned to Silva and smiled.

"A catpanion is the official title of a catgirl who is in a romantic relationship with a human. It's a lot like marriage, but because of the nature of catgirl and human relationships, it isn't held to the same standards." Akari paused.

"So it's different from when someone is your guardian?" Silva tilted her head, cat ears twitching as her tail swayed back and forth.

"Very different." Akari nodded. "A guardian is basically like a foster parent. Becoming someone's catpanion is the same thing as declaring your love for them and your intention to remain with them through sickness and health until death do you part."

Silva finally seemed to understand what becoming a catpanion was. Her eyes went wide and her tail stood straight and became bristly. She glanced over at Chris, her cheeks turning a dark shade of scarlet that complimented her porcelain complexion before she looked away.

Her reaction seemed to amuse Akari—who smiled—and Tanner—who laughed—but Chris felt a little concerned. He didn't know what she was thinking, but he also didn't want her to feel pressured into thinking she needed to become his catpanion since they were living together. She had just mentioned repaying her debt to him, so he felt it was a viable concern. Maybe he should talk to her about this? He sighed. This whole situation was troublesome.

They stayed for a little while after dinner and then left. Akari told them they were welcome to come over whenever they wanted, and she even insisted that Silva should come over again. Silva gave her an uncertain smile before saying she would consider it. Chris was sure she still didn't know how to deal with Akari, but she was at least not as reticent to speak with her as before.

As they sat on the bus, Chris frowned when he noticed that Silva was sitting a lot further from him than usual. During their journey to Tanner's house, she had plastered herself to him, but now she was sitting with a seat between them. It was still close enough to be considered close. However, it was further than it had been before.

"Is something wrong?" Chris asked.

"N-nyot at all!" Silva squeaked.

"You've picked up an accent." When Silva held a hand to her mouth, Chris sighed. "Is it about what Akari said? You know, about what it means to be a catpanion?" Silva's silence was telling. "Look, you don't need to worry about something like that. I'd never force you to become my catpanion, and I don't want you thinking you have to become my catpanion to repay any perceived debt."

Chris wanted to make sure she understood that he wasn't expecting anything in return for helping her. He was someone who was training to become a catgirl doctor. He wouldn't have wanted to become one if he was the kind of person who would help a catgirl and expect her to repay her debts at a later time.

"I understand," Silva said in a soft voice.

"Good." Chris released a deep breath, then reached out and patted her hand before withdrawing it. "Please just treat me as you always have. Don't worry about anything except getting healthy."

"Okay," Silva said.

As silence elapsed between them, Chris looked out the window, watching as the cars went past. Even though he said he didn't want her to worry about becoming his catpanion, he would admit, if only to himself, that he didn't mind the idea. However, if it did happen, he didn't want it to be for the wrong reasons.

He wondered when life had become so complicated.

chapter 7

Chris had come to the conclusion that something was eating away at Silva. He couldn't figure out what, but it felt like something was bothering her. For the past several days, a feeling of helplessness had come over him as he watched the catgirl he lived with suffering in silence. Perhaps she didn't know what was wrong herself, perhaps she just didn't want him to know, but whatever was going on, Chris was getting sick and tired of not being able to do a single thing to help her.

That was why he had decided to ask someone who might be able to help him figure this out.

"You… want to ask me if something is wrong with Silva?" Anastasia looked at Chris like he'd sprouted a head from ass, wings from his back, and grew a unicorn horn.

"Yes… is there something wrong with that?" Chris carefully asked when he saw her expression. He didn't think he'd said anything wrong, but at the same time, women were a breed he had never claimed to understand.

Anastasia rubbed her face as she leaned back in her seat. They were in the lecture hall for their Catgirl Biology class. As usual, he and Anastasia were sitting together.

Chris had come to her to ask for her advice, but Anastasia seemed reluctant to give it for some reason. He wasn't exactly sure why. Well, he had some ideas, but he believed those ideas were the stuff of arrogance and wishful thinking.

"Well… there isn't anything wrong with asking me for help, per se…" Anastasia replied with what sounded like great reluctance. "However, I'm not really sure what I can help you with. I don't even know this catgirl you live with, you know?"

"I-I know that, but I don't really know what to do." Chris placed his hands on his thighs and clenched them. "Every time I ask Silva if something is wrong, she tells me nothing is wrong, but I can tell that she's burdened by something."

"How can you tell?" asked Anastasia, looking curious despite her previous statements.

"Whenever I go outside to run errands, whether that's simple grocery shopping or going to the kickboxing center, Silva always demands to come along with me."

"I'm not sure I see the problem here."

Chris gave the befuddled Anastasia a smile. "Despite the fact that she constantly demands to come with me, every time we go outside, she has panic attacks. It wasn't so bad at first, but the more she goes outside, the worse it gets. Despite this, she continues to push herself into going outside. I don't understand why she's doing this."

"Ah." Anastasia's eyes lit up as if she finally understood.

Chris ran a hand through his hair. "It's not so bad when we just go grocery shopping, so long as I avoid entering isles with other people, but it becomes really bad when she goes to the kickboxing center with me. Several people aside from myself have tried talking to her, and she freaks out every time. It was especially bad when one man tried to hit on her while I was in the shower…"

A shudder ran through Chris as he remembered what happened. He'd only been gone for five minutes, but in those five minutes, Silva had a huge panic attack when someone tried to talk her up. He didn't know what had been said. He honestly didn't care. What mattered was that Silva had run out of the kickboxing center and climbed a tree. He'd found her terrified and shivering like kitten who'd become stuck on a branch and couldn't get down.

"She's also been having trouble sleeping, gets stomach aches, and will occasionally freak out." Chris furrowed his brow as he continued listing all the problems Silva was having. "I thought things were going well because she'd taken a liking to me and wasn't exhibiting any problems at first, but more problems have been showing up the longer she lives with me. I'm wondering if… maybe I should let someone else take care of her." He paused to look at the pensive Anastasia. "Do you think I might be the problem?"

Biting her lip, Anastasia looked like she was seriously considering his issue. He waited, feeling his stomach twisting into knots, as she slowly shook her head.

"I don't think you are the problem," she said at last. "You've mentioned all the issues she's been having, but you haven't said anything about her actively avoiding you or disliking you."

"Well, that is true, but…"

"Have you ever tried to touch her and she flinched away?" asked Anastasia.

"Well, no…"

"Has she ever shied away from you when you're with her."

"No."

"Then it's probably not you." Anastasia concluded her theory with a nod. "It sounds to me like what's eating at her has to do with something entirely separate from you."

"Then what could it be?" Chris wondered out loud.

Anastasia shrugged. "I honestly have no idea, but you said she was abused, so maybe she's experience flashbacks from when she was abused. I've heard some people who have just been through a traumatic experience don't show symptoms of it until much later. It could be that the situation she was in before meeting you has finally hit her, and it's causing her to relive her past trauma."

That was something he hadn't considered, but now that he was, Chris was kicking himself over it. He had taken psychology courses during high school so he could have those credits. Thinking back on it, he remembered several lectures that dealt with veteran soldiers who, upon returning from the war, would act perfectly normal for a while as they tried to return to how their lives used to be, but then would begin experiencing flashbacks and suffer from PTSD months or even years later.

Chris wanted to ask Anastasia more questions. However, Professor Shinomiya chose that moment to enter class.

Most of the class became silent as the woman stepped onto the podium. She placed her purse and a water bottle on the desk, grabbed the remote, and flipped on the monitor. An image was projected on the screen. It was of a catgirl, but this image showed off the different muscle groups. It was a muscle diagram.

"Today, we're going to go over the muscle groups found in a catgirl and what differences they have with humans." The woman paused and turned her gaze onto a pair of students who were still talking. "Would you two like to finish your conversation outside of my class? I can kick you out if you want." At her words, the pair of men instantly shut their mouths. "Now, as I was saying, we're going to go over the muscle groups found in catgirls."

She pressed a button on her remote, which caused the muscle diagram to suddenly transform into a 3D representation. Chris realized it was actually a video. The 3D model began rotating, showing the catgirl body from every conceivable angle.

"As you can see from this diagram, a catgirl's muscle systems seems, at first glance, to be nearly identical to those of a human's," Professor Shinomiya began. "However, when you look more closely, you'll realize that their musculature is actually quite a bit different from those of a human's. Of course, the most obvious examples of these differences are their ears and tail. Humans don't even have those. However, we're going to take a closer look at the things we can't see with our eyes. Namely, today we will be talking about the heart."

Professor Shinomiya reached out and grabbed her water bottle, undoing the lid and taking a drink before she set it back down. During that time, only the sound of pencils scribbling against paper and Anastasia's fingers hitting the keyboard echoed around them.

"For every beat our human heart takes, a typical catgirl's heart will beat three times. It works a lot more than our own. A cat's heart, including arteries, capillaries, and veins are finely-tuned to control the amount of blood circulating in the body at any one time. Also closely controlled are the blood plasma contents, including sugar, hormones, salts, acidity, and concentration. Blood pressure is another component of a healthy cardiovascular system that requires constant monitoring by the body. Considering all the delicate nerve signals, fine coordination of muscle contractions, and hormonal messages needed to keep everything working just right, there are surprisingly few problems with catgirls from a statistical point of view, but that doesn't mean heart disease can't occur."

Professor Shinomiya's lecture continued for the entire period. During this time, Chris thought about Silva and what might be bugging her. He now understood that she was suffering from some kind of PTSD. However, was it just

PTSD or was there something else that was also bothering her?

He really wanted to know the answer.

✳✳✳

Chris only knew one veteran. Tanner. The man was currently on the reserves, but he'd experienced the war in Iraq from the very beginning back in 2003 all the way to when it ended in 2011. If anyone knew about people who had post-traumatic stress disorder, Chris thought for sure it would be him.

"You want to know if Silva has PTSD?" Tanner looked at Chris like he'd said something dumb, but he didn't think his question had been stupid at all.

"I think she might have something similar," he confirmed. "Post-traumatic stress disorder is a health condition triggered by terrifying events. I don't think there are many things more terrifying than being raped."

"That is true," Tanner admitted.

It was about one hour after Chris's exercise, and he had stayed behind specifically to ask Tanner this question. All around them were people exercising. Some were doing cardio in the cardio section, others were pounding away at the punching bags, and a few people were sparring in the ring.

The scent of sweat and gym equipment was heavy in the air, and the sounds of fists thudding against objects resounded all around them.

Tanner rubbed his jaw as he thought about this. "I do know some people who have PTSD, but it's always triggered by something similar to the memory. Like your catgirl for example. Let's say she did have PTSD from what that scumbag did to her. If that was the case, don't you think she would flinch away from you whenever you tried to touch her? Also, if she did have PTSD, she would go out of her way to avoid situations that involve going outside and dealing with people, but instead of doing that, she has been forcing herself out of the house. That sort of behavior is the exact opposite of someone with PTSD."

"That... that is true," Chris admitted. "So you think it isn't PTSD?"

The thought made him frown. If it wasn't PTSD that was the problem, then it meant Chris was back to square one. He pinched the bridge of his nose.

"I don't think that is the problem, but I do think the problem is related to what happened to her." Chris remained silent as Tanner looked off into the distance, his eyes growing slightly vacant. "You know, during the war, I saw a lot of friends die. Sometimes they would be lost to gunfire, sometimes they would die after stepping on a landmine, and some even died in my arms. I lost too many friends to count."

Tanner had never spoken about his past before. Chris had never asked because he respected the man's right to his privacy. He assumed the man simply hadn't wanted to say anything because of how much it hurt, but as Chris imagined the scenes Tanner spoke of playing out in his mind, he now realized that his trainer had also been silent so as not to disturb others with the imagery his words invoked.

What Chris imagined as the man spoke of his experiences was not pleasant.

"After surviving so many battles and watching as others didn't, I began to wonder: Why me? Why was I the only one who kept surviving? Why did everyone around me have to constantly die? It became so bad that I asked my commanding officer to send me out alone because I was afraid everyone else would die if they came with me. Of course, he didn't do that, and many people died, but I continued to survive. I eventually began to think I was cursed to watch all the people I became friends die, which led to me isolating myself from others."

"You're talking about survivor's guilt, right?" A pensive expression appeared on Chris's face as he felt a deep niggling in his chest, like someone was slowly digging out his organs with a knife. "I don't think that's it either. I mean, she's not isolating herself. Silva is—"

Chris paused as he had a sudden epiphany. At the same time, Tanner gave him a pained smile.

"There are many ways people deal with survivor's guilt," he said. "Some people try to avoid everything because they don't believe they deserve happiness... other people try to punish themselves for the same reason."

After hearing what Tanner had to say, Chris could do nothing except race out of the kickboxing center and head back home as quickly as his legs could carry him.

It was still chilly. The cool air caused his chest to ache as he breathed it in and ran. Yet that was a trivial experience compared to the tightness in his chest. His worry for Silva overrode everything else and consumed his mind as he ran all the way to his apartment, opened the door, and ran inside.

"Silva?" he called out after getting home.

No one answered him, which was odd, since Silva would normally get up from the couch and greet him with a smile, but the TV wasn't on right now and she wasn't sitting on the couch. Dropping his bag onto the floor, Chris headed toward his bedroom. However, she wasn't in there either.

Now feeling panic settle in his stomach, Chris stared around his empty apartment and wondered where she'd gone. Had she... run away? Would she do that? Chris closed his eyes to keep himself from losing it. If she'd run away, he might not be able to find her depending on how far she'd gone. There was also the worry that someone else, someone with ill-intentions, might have picked her up. A catgirl wandering the streets alone was like painting a target on one's back.

"Silva?!" He called out again, louder this time.

A sudden splash caused Chris to turn his head toward the bathroom door. Running into the bathroom, which Silva never locked when she was bathing, he burst inside and found her. Silva was in the bath. Heat rose from the tub as she lay there. However, it looked like she had stayed in too long and gotten dizzy from the heat. Her body had sunken into the water and she appeared to be on the verge of drowning in the bath!

"Oh, crap! Silva!"

Chris did his best to rescue the girl before she could drown in the bathtub.

****

Chris was making dinner. This was as much to settle his nerves as it was because he needed sustenance. The situation with Silva nearly drowning had left him in a state of shock. Had he actually gotten home later, it was possible Silva would have drown in his bathtub. A chill ran down his spine when this thought occurred to him.

He had heard that it was possible to drown in the tub, which happened primarily due to someone suffering from their blood pressure dropping. Still, that was the kind of stuff you heard of happening in movies and to heavy drinkers who take baths while intoxicated. He never expected it to happen to Silva.

Dinner that evening was honey garlic salmon that had been pan seared and coated in a sweet and savory honey garlic sauce. The sauce was made from garlic, honey, and soy sauce to give it a unique flavor. Of course, he made Silva's sauce separate from his own. He had added the dietary supplements she was supposed to take into the sauce for her. These supplements had no flavor, so he was trying to make them easier for her to consume.

"Here you are," Chris said as he wandered into the living room with two plates in hand. He set one plate in front of Silva as she sat on the chair in front of the dinner table with her knees curled into her chest, then set the other plate in front of where he sat.

"Thank you," Silva said in a soft voice that was barely above a whisper.

Chris tried to give her a smile, but he wasn't sure he succeeded. "You're welcome."

Dinner was a silent affair this time. Chris and Silva would normally speak during dinner… well, Chris would tell her about his day while Silva listened and asked some questions, but it was often filled with more noise than this. The only thing Chris could hear now was the chirping of crickets, or maybe that was his imagination.

After dinner, Chris cleaned off the plates, then took Silva by the hand and led her over to the couch. She didn't resist him at all. He remembered Tanner's words that when someone had PTSD, they avoided whatever triggered that emotional response. Given what happened to her, how she'd been abused by a man, he took this as proof that she wasn't suffering from PTSD but something else.

"Silva." Chris knelt before the catgirl as she sat with her hands on her lap, staring up into her vivid eyes. "Do you feel guilty that you escaped from your abuser and the others didn't?"

Silva's eyes went wide. "I…"

"I've been thinking about this a lot. For the past several days, you've been really worrying me, and I was wondering if I did something wrong."

"You didn't!" Silva suddenly shouted, but then she quieted down and looked at her hands. "You did nothing wrong. You've taken such good care of me… but that's the problem." Chris said nothing as Silva struggled to keep a lid on her emotions. He wanted her to tell him what was wrong, but he didn't want to prod and force her into speaking. She needed to speak on her own time. "You've been so good to me, letting me stay here, feeding me delicious food, and not even asking for anything in return. For the first time since Grams died, I've been really happy, but everyone else is... I... I don't deserve to have these feelings!"

"Because of the other catgirls?" Chris asked.

Silva nodded as tears began streaming down her cheeks. Her arms trembled from the weight of her own emotions.

"When I escaped, the others were still locked up in their cages. Only Kuro had also been released because she shared a cage with me, but she had thrown herself at our guardian and told me to run. I didn't... even look back! I ran! I left her all alone! As I was running up the stairs, I heard gunfire! But even after that, I didn't look back and just kept running! I left all those other catgirls to fend for themselves and ran away like a coward!"

As Silva finally poured out all the emotions she'd been feeling, Chris silently shut his eyes and struggled to keep a lid on his own feelings. Listening to Silva as she cried was heartrending. He couldn't even begin to imagine what she was going through, having never gone through it himself, but that was also why he believed she needed to let all this out.

"Someone like me doesn't deserve to be happy," Silva finished as she tried to wipe her face, only for more to tears to create streaks down her face and drip off her chin.

Chris wondered if there was anything he could do to help Silva with her emotions. After a moment, he reached up and placed his hands on her cheeks. Silva stiffened, but he leaned in until their foreheads were touching and began wiping away her tears with his thumb, even if it was a futile gesture.

Chris was honestly a little worried about doing something so intimate. While they'd been close before, he'd made sure to never initiate any intimate contact for fear of triggering a traumatic experience. However, right now, his concern was over helping this girl understand that she had nothing to feel guilty about.

"You're a very silly girl," Chris said at last.

"W-what?" Silva looked confused. Her big, beautiful, heterochromatic eyes blinked several times.

"Kuro attacked that man so you could escape, didn't she? That means she wanted you to leave and not look back. She doesn't sound like the kind of person who would blame you for what happened," Chris said.

"But—"

"And also, if you really do feel guilty, then instead of punishing yourself by forcing yourself into situations you aren't comfortable with, don't you think your time and effort would be better spent helping rescue the other catgirls?"

As he proposed this idea to her, Silva went silent, her cute nose scrunching up in confusion, hope, and pain. Chris continued to massage her cheeks with his thumb. It felt a little weird to caress her cheeks. If he had been doing this with a human woman, he would have been able to feel her ears, but Silva's ears were on top of her head. She didn't have human ears, which meant the place where he'd normally feel them was barren.

"How… can I help them?" she said at last.

"Right now, the police are investigating this man's whereabouts," Chris said. "Until they find something, there's not a whole lot we can do personally. However, once they do find this person, you can help them by making sure he can never do what he did to you and the other catgirls again. You can also help the other catgirls once they are free. I'll help you."

"You will?" Silva asked, sniffling.

"I will," Chris confirmed. "So no more feeling guilty, no more punishing yourself, and no more tears… okay?"

Silva nodded and Chris slowly withdrew his head from hers. He took a deep breath and held it.

Given what she was going through, Chris didn't think this one conversation would be enough to help Silva overcome her issues, but he promised himself that he would be there for her. If she stumbled or fell, he'd help pick her back up so she could keep moving forward.

"Do you feel a little better?" asked Chris.

"I do." Silva rubbed her nose with the back of her hand. Her eyes were bloodshot, red, and puffy, but she still smiled at him. "Thank you."

"You're welcome."

Chris sat down on the couch next to Silva and turned on the TV. He let her choose what to watch, which ended up being a cooking show featuring a famous chef who he actually knew. Gordon Ramsay. This particular show wasn't the man's infamous Hell's Kitchen, which was the show where Gordon Ramsay verbally tore into chefs competing in his cooking competition. It looked like this one featured kids cooking desserts.

As he sat there, Silva slowly fell into his side, her head resting on his shoulder. He glanced at her, but she didn't seem to have realized what she was doing. Her heterochromatic eyes glowed as the light from the television played off them.

A catgirl's eyes were always quite vivid. Like a regular cat, catgirls had a layer called the tapetum lucidum just behind their retina. This layer reflected light. Cats, dogs, dear, and other nocturnal animals had great night vision because whatever the photoreceptor cells in their retina didn't catch hit the tapetum lucidum and took a second pass at the retina again.

Since the tapetum lucidum was a great deal more reflective than the retina, the redness was washed away by whatever materials made up the reflective layer. It was the lack of this layer that caused humans to have shining eyes only in photos and not when being hit in the face with a flashlight. A catgirl's eyes were, just like the heart, one of the many differences between a human and a catgirl.

As these thoughts flashed through his mind, Chris looked back at the cooking show Silva was so fixated on. He wondered what about cooking shows fascinated her so much. However, he didn't question this. Given the state he found her in, it was clear that she had been starved during her time with her abuser.

Without conscious thought, he slowly reached around the girl and wrapped his arm around her waist. Silva jumped a little, as if surprised, but then she relaxed against him.

Like that, they spent the rest of their night on the couch until Silva fell asleep.

chapter 8

Sweat stained Chris's clothing and drenched his body as he continuously punched and kicked the punching bag hanging from the ceiling without relent. Left. Right. He thrust his left fist out, rotating his whole body to put as much power into it as he could. A satisfying thud rang out as he slammed his fist into the punching bag, which rattled. Then he spun on the balls of his feet, lifted his left leg, and slammed into the bag with the phalanges of his foot.

"Ha... ha..."

His breathing had grown heavy as he worked, coming out in ragged gasps. Yet even then Chris did not stop for anything. He kept hitting the punching bag as though he was trying to beat it so hard the sand filling spilled out.

He didn't just throw heavy punches. Chris also threw several short and fast jabs. Each jab caused the punching bag to shake. He'd launch two swift jabs followed by a left or right hook, then deliver a punishing blow with all his weight before moving into a variety of different kicks.

"And… time!"

As Tanner's voice echoed to him, Chris stopped working, heaving several deep breaths as a sharp pain filled his chest. He stretched his shoulders, pulling them back, then hunching them forward, and then pulling them back again. He did this several times. Finally, after the ache in his chest ebbed, he glanced at Tanner.

The man was standing right beside him, dressed in standard black workout shorts and a sleeveless shirt that showed off his ridiculously muscled body. With the light reflecting off his dark skin, he looked even more ripped than normal.

"You've been at this for a full 30 minutes," Tanner said at last, grinning. "That's pretty good. Most people don't last more than 20 at most."

"Good to know." Chris's breathing had grown a lot more even now. As he rotated his shoulders, he glanced at Tanner. "What's next, Captain?"

"Next we're just going to do basic exercise. Let's start with some crunches."

They moved over to the simple exercise mats, and when Chris laid down, Tanner sat with his knees on Chris's toes, keeping his feet in place, then held up his hands, which were covered in a pair of boxing pads. The pads were mostly white and black, but there was a red circle in the center. It looked like a target.

Chris began doing crunches, but they were a bit different from normal crunches. He came up, punched both pads with a simple left and right jab, went back down, then repeated the process. The muscles in his stomach were burning as he moved, especially when he held his upright position to punch. He kept working, however, until he eventually did 200 crunches.

Push ups came next. Once again, they were different from normal. They were called Spider-Man Push ups. He lifted one leg and moved it out while he was going down, then brought it back in and lifted the other leg to do the same thing. It worked out his core and hips alongside his chest. He could only do 50 of these, but that was still pretty good by his standards.

Chris spent another half an hour working out his body, and by the time he finished, it felt like he'd lost all his fluids through his pores. He grabbed the water bottle he'd kept with him and deeply drank the liquid. It wasn't water that was inside, but Gatorade to help replenish his electrolytes.

Now that he was done with his exercises, Chris sat off to the side and watched the others for a moment. He planned to go home soon, but he wanted to rest first. His muscles ached.

"So it's been about two weeks since you began living with that catgirl of yours," Tanner said as he sat down beside Chris. "How's that working out?"

"It's a lot better now, I think," Chris said. "Silva is no longer trying to punish herself like she did before. She doesn't go out of the house as much because of that, but she does go shopping with me. She says it's because she wants to get better. I'm still a little worried. However, so long as she's doing this because she wants to get over her fears and not because she's punishing herself, I'll support her."

"That's good. I'm glad to hear the girl isn't beating herself up anymore. And how about your relationship?" asked Tanner. "Has that changed at all?"

Chris took a deep breath. "I haven't made a move on her, if that's what you're asking."

"Not attracted to her?"

"That's not it." He shook his head. "Ever since she gained a healthy weight, Silva has become almost unbearably attractive."

"Then why haven't you made a move?" Tanner pressed.

"Because of her previous guardian." Chris ran a hand through his sweaty hair. "Her previous guardian raped her. That's not something you just get over. Even if she's not afraid of me, I'm afraid that if I make a move, she'll suffer a relapse."

"That's understandable." Tanner nodded. "Speaking of, has there been any news on her previous guardian?"

Chris shook his head. "If there has, the police haven't contacted me about it"

"Well, he might have run." Tanner scratched his head and glanced at the ceiling. "Guys like that are cowards. They always run at the first sign of trouble."

"That doesn't surprise me."

Chris spoke with Tanner for a little while longer, but the man couldn't spend all his time talking to him. He was training several other people. When the man stood up and began working with one of his other regulars, Chris also stood up and traveled toward the showers. He'd take a quick rinse and head home.

***

"I'm about to get started on my chicken cacciatore, and the first thing I want to do is season my four chicken breasts and four chicken thighs…"

Silva's mouth watered as she watched the woman on the screen give instructions on how to make a chicken cacciatore, which was a food she had never tried before. This cooking channel had become one of her favorites. She loved watching all the different kinds of food that were cooked.

However, as the woman continued cooking, the sound of a door unlocking made her ears twitch. She scrambled to her feet as the door opened and tried not to dash toward it. As Chris appeared, Silva's heart thundered in her chest as she fast-walked over to him.

"I'm back," Chris said.

"Welcome home," Silva answered as she pressed herself forward, knocking into him.

Chris grunted as he took a few steps back, but then he reached out and began caressing her hair and ears. It felt really good. Her body felt like it was melting as he touched her ears, which flicked every so often under his ministrations. A purr emerged from the back of her throat as she rubbed her face into his chest and took in several deep breaths.

It felt like his scent was engulfing her. As the masculine smell that was unique to Chris entered her nose, Silva's body heated up. Her heart felt like it was beating out of her chest as an incredible warmth raced through her body, particularly her lower body.

The feeling of his hard muscles against her skin was searing. Chris had a very strong body. She longed to have him wrap his arms around her, but she also wanted something more.

Because she only came up to Chris's chest, Silva had to lean on her tiptoes to place her nose in the crook of his neck, but once she did, she took in a deep breath and nuzzled against his skin. She tentatively stuck out a tongue. She wanted to lick him, to taste him. She wanted… wanted…

"Silva? Are you okay?"

"Huh?"

It was only several seconds later, when Chris called her name, that Silva realized she'd been pressing her entire body against his, nearly plastering herself to him.

"MEOW!"

In shock, Silva leapt back and stared at Chris. His expression was perplexed as he stared back. Silva felt blood rush to her cheeks as embarrassment filled her, but she took several deep breaths and tried to calm down. There was a raging fire inside of her now. She wanted to just rub herself against Chris and mark him with her scent, but she did her best to stifle it.

"Silva?"

"Y-yes?!" Silva said, her voice several decibels louder than she'd intended.

"Are you feeling all right?" asked Chris.

"I'm fine." Silva looked away. If she looked at Chris any longer, she feared she might attack him. "A-anyway, how was school and the gym?"

"It was good."

Chris shifted his backpack and gym bag over his shoulders as he slipped off his shoes and walked toward his bedroom. Silva followed after him. However, that proved to be a mistake. The gym bag had a very strong smell coming from it, and Silva found herself taking several deep breaths as she leaned forward to smell it. Her body grew even hotter.

"What are you doing?" asked Chris.

"N-nyothing!"

Silva backed away and shook her head, but Chris continued to stare at her as he set down his backpack and gym bag. There was a frown on his face. She glanced away and took several steps back, afraid that he might have figured out there was something wrong with her.

After a moment or two, Chris seemed to decide there was nothing wrong. He unzipped the gym bag. Silva's legs instantly weakened as Chris's smell pervaded the entire room. She licked her lips as, out of the corner of her eye, she watched him remove his gym clothes and place them inside of the dirty clothes bin in the corner closest to the closet.

"Anyway, you asked about class? It was pretty informative this time," Chris continued. "We learned about some of the key differences between catgirls and humans. Catgirls are like a combination between cat and human, and their internal organs are a mix between the two. Did you know that catgirls have a vomeronasal organ? It's also known as the Jacobson's organ. It's located in the back of a catgirl's mouth and helps them pick up scents. This is part of the reason catgirls have a stronger sense of smell than humans."

"Is… is that so? I didn't know that."

Silva blinked several times as she listened to Chris talk, but it sounded like his voice was coming from a vast distance away. She tried to listen. However, it was becoming harder to even focus on his words the longer she remained in that room, the longer she continued to smell him.

"I didn't either." Chris seemed oblivious to her plight as he continued talking. "I used to think I knew everything there was to know about catgirls because I lived with one for several years, but ever since attending college, I'm discovering more and more things I never knew."

It was fortunate for Silva that Chris soon left the bedroom after putting his clothes and school supplies away. She was able to breathe a sigh of relief once they left the bedroom. She made sure the door was closed as well, which brought her a slight stare from Chris, but he didn't say anything about that.

"I'm about to get started on dinner. Do you want anything specific?"

"Chicken cacciatore!" Silva answered immediately.

Chris gave her an amused smile that caused her cheeks to flush. "I'm not sure if I have all the ingredients for that, but let me see what's in my fridge."

Just as Chris had said, he didn't have all of the ingredients necessary for a true chicken cacciatore. He was missing the chicken thighs and several seasonings. However, he did have two large chicken breast, which he seasoned with salt and black pepper before lightly coating it in flour. He sautéd the chicken breasts until they were a nice brown color, then added freshly squeezed lemon juice and capers to give it more flavor. He didn't have any bell peppers or the necessary ingredients for a sauce, so he threw together a salad with a light dressing.

Silva watched him work, her tail waving back and forth as she admired the way he moved about the kitchen. Something about seeing him cook was attractive. It caused her breathing to grow heavy, but she quickly shook her head and tried to distract herself by moving to the couch and watching the cooking show again.

When dinner was ready, the two of them sat down and ate. During this time, Chris told her about his day, about all the things he had done in class and at the gym. Silva normally listened attentively as he talked, but today it was hard. She kept thinking about Chris's cooking, and his scent, and how she wanted to rub her body against him.

"Seriously. Are you sure your okay?" asked Chris. "You keep spacing out on me."

"Huh?! Y-yes, I am fine!" Silva squealed when she realized Chris had caught her staring again. "I've just been… distracted."

"Distracted by what?"

"Uh… well…"

Silva didn't know what to say. She couldn't tell him that she was thinking of rubbing her body all over him. The very thought left her feeling flushed. She tried to come up with something, but she kept drawing a blank.

"Just… um… stuff."

"Stuff?" Chris raised an eyebrow.

Silva looked at her now cleaned off plate. "Stuff."

"Well, okay…"

Chris seemed to realize something as he dropped the subject.

After dinner, Chris cleaned off their plates and the pan he used to cook in before grabbing his backpack from his bedroom and sitting on the couch next to Silva. This was how their day normally went. He would do his homework in the living room while she watched TV. Sometimes she would watch him work. However, even though she could read, she couldn't understand all the complicated stuff he wrote, so she more often than not didn't pay attention.

Chris did eye Silva again as she sat as far from him as possible. However, he didn't say anything as he got started on his homework. It looked like math. Silva only understood the basics of math, like addition and subtraction. All the complicated numbers and words lining the pages Chris was working on confused her.

He eventually finished his homework and began watching TV with her. They didn't speak much, but both occasionally commented on the show they were watching. Since they were both watching TV, Silva had switched the show from the cooking channel to Netflix. They were watching a Netflix original called *The Seven Deadly Sins*. It was an interesting show about a princess who wanted to find the kingdom's most notorious criminals to help her stop the knights of her kingdom, who had staged coup d'etat and taken over the kingdom.

"I don't really understand," Silva confessed. "Aren't the knights supposed to be good guys? Why are they fighting against the princess?"

"There is a reason for that, but you actually don't learn about it until much later." Chris scratched his chin, and Silva found herself wishing he'd scratch her chin. "At the start, Elizabeth thinks the reason is because the knights have become corrupted by the power they wield. We don't learn until much later that the Holy Knights are actually being manipulated by demons. Actually, I don't think we even learn this until season 2."

"Season 2?"

Chris smiled at her. "Just keep watching."

Silva nodded and watched the show with Chris. They only watched a few episodes before it became late. Night was settling as the sun went down and the moon came out. When it reached that late, Chris and Silva went into the bathroom to prepare for bed.

Chris had done more shopping for her, and Silva now had several necessities like an automatic toothbrush, a shower cap for her hair, several soft towels, and soap and shampoo meant specifically for catgirls. Chris had even bought her a very fine brush for her hair and tail.

After they finished brushing, flossing, and rinsing out their mouths, Silva went into Chris's bedroom while Chris went into the living room. She laid on the bed and tried to sleep. However, it was impossible with Chris's scent pervading the air.

Silva tossed and turned as the heat in her body rose. Her breathing grew heavy as she reached out and grabbed her small breasts. Her nipples had grown hard. She pinched and twisted them, biting her lip as she struggled to contain her moaning. As she played with her chest, her crotch became wet. Without hesitation, as if something had suddenly possessed her, Silva slipped her hands down her pants and pressed a finger to her pussy lips.

"Hyk!"

Eyes clenched shut, Silva gritted her teeth as an intense surge of pleasure rocked her body. She rubbed her wet vagina, petting it like Chris would pet her head. The wetness flowing from her entrance increased as her stroking became more vigorous.

"Meow. Mreow!"

Saliva leaked from her lips as she continued playing with herself, yet for whatever reason, no matter how much she rubbed herself, she couldn't find any release. She needed to do something more drastic.

Climbing off the bed, Silva went over to the dirty clothes bin and grabbed the gym clothes Chris had deposited. She brought the clothing to her face and breathed in his scent. This overpowering smell was the cause of her arousal.

Silva climbed back onto the bed and removed her pink pajama bottoms. She also slid her panties down her hips. With one hand holding Chris's clothing to her nose so she could breathe in his scent, she placed the other hand between her legs and began playing with herself.

"Chris… Chris… mreow!"

She moaned as the intense feelings rocking her body jolted her like bolts of lightning. Silva turned over in bed, stuck her butt in the air, and pressed her face against Chris's shirt as she inserted a finger into her vagina. She rocked her hips as her tail stood on end. The sensations inside of her as she plunged her fingers into her vagina were so intense that she had to bite Chris's clothing to keep her cries muffled. She could feel something coming. Her body was growing even more hot as an incredible pressure welled up inside of her stomach.

Finally, it happened.

Silva's toes clenched as her hips and thighs tightened. An incredible release of energy flowed through her body as her mind went white with pleasure. Something warm and wet flowed down her thighs. This feeling lasted for several seconds before it disappeared.

"Ha… Ha… Mreow…"

Silva let her butt slid back down, her left hand still firmly pressed to her crotch, finger still inside. Her body shuddered with slight aftershocks as her mind grew slightly numb.

After awhile, Silva recovered enough to realize what she'd done. Her entire body felt like it had heated up with embarrassment. She climbed off the bed, her knees wobbling, and was about to put Chris's shirt back in the dirty clothes bin, but she froze the moment she turned to face the door.

"Ah… Chris… this is… this isn't what it looks like…"

Standing in the doorway, staring at her with an expression that was a mixture of shock and something else that she couldn't place was Chris.

***

It was late at night. The moon had risen high above the Earth, casting its soft glow upon the world. Moonbeams leaked in through the window. Chris and Silva were sitting on the couch in the living room again. However, neither of them spoke. Neither of them were able to speak.

Chris was replaying what happened in his mind. He'd woken up after hearing strange sounds coming from his bedroom. Having recognized Silva's voice, he'd grown worried that maybe she was having a nightmare, but then he'd rushed into the bedroom and caught Silva masturbating. Not only had he been given a perfect view of her small ass as she fingered herself, but he'd noticed her smelling his shirt as she masturbated.

The moment he'd seen this, all the little things he'd noticed from Silva today had struck him like a bolt of lightning, and he'd finally realized what the problem was.

He looked at Silva, who refused to meet his gaze. She was sitting as far from him as possible. Her cheeks were redder than he'd ever seen them. Meanwhile, her tail flicked from side to side in an agitated fashion as her ears bristled. He didn't think she was upset like these mannerisms usually indicated, but she was probably embarrassed.

In the past two weeks since she had begun living with him, Silva's body had filled out a good deal. Her ribs no longer showed, her thighs were a little plumper, and her arms didn't look like twigs. She was still incredibly thin. However, her species weren't known for their size to begin with. They had gone back to Doctor Medisson for a checkup two days ago and Silva's weight had reached 106 pounds, which was considered the ideal weight for her species.

"You are in heat, aren't you?" Chris asked. The redness on Silva's cheeks deepened, which he didn't think he was possible.

"I… um… yes. I am."

Silva looked anywhere but at Chris, which forced him to withhold a sigh.

"Is this the first time you've been in heat?"

Silva hesitated, but then shook her head. "No. Um, this is my fourth time. W-when I was younger and started going into heat, Grams would take me to a Catgirl Hospital and take the pill to stop them, so I've never... had to deal with it until today."

Chris was a little shocked. Catgirls began going into heat when they were 16 years-old. If Silva had experienced four mating periods in her life, then it meant she was 20 years-old, which meant she was actually older than him by at least a year or so. He honestly thought she was younger.

"I-I'm sorry," Silva said. Chris didn't know why she was apologizing, but then she covered her face with her hands and continued. "You must... think I'm weird. A catgirl sniffing your clothes and touching herself is weird, right?"

Chris couldn't deny that it was a little weird, but...

"It's not like I'm bothered by it," he said at last.

"What?"

Silva removed her hands from her face and stared at him. Chris looked away, feeling his own cheeks rise a little.

"I said I don't mind," he said, then continued. "I mean... it was shocking, yes, but seeing you like that was... it was kind of hot."

"W-was it really?" Silva looked shocked, but when Chris nodded, a relieved smile lit up her face. She placed a hand against her chest as if to calm her beating heart. "Then… um… does that mean you find me attractive?"

When Chris had first met Silva, she was quite literally all skin and bones. She hadn't been what he could call attractive because of how unhealthy she looked. However, as she filled out, even though she remained thin, her body had become a lot more beautiful. The bruises had long since faded, leaving behind healthy white skin. Her thighs, hips, and chest were bigger than before, though her chest still wasn't even a handful. That said…

"I think you are very pretty," Chris confirmed with a nod.

Silva placed her hands on her cheeks. As she did, Chris scratched his head as he tried to figure out what he should do now. He'd learned about a catgirl's mating period in school, so he knew there were only a few ways to deal with this, but he wasn't a breeder. Breeders were people whose entire job was to have sex with catgirls for a living to help them deal with their mating periods. It was a very specific job that required men to pass a number of tests.

Of course, he didn't have to be a breeder to have sex with a catgirl, but on the other hand, he wasn't the type who would just sleep with anyone under the sun. If he went through with the idea he was thinking about, it would change the entire dynamics of their relationship.

"How long… have you been in heat?" asked Chris.

"About... two days... I think," Silva answered, though she didn't sound sure. "I'm not exactly sure when it started, but for awhile now, I've been getting really excited by your scent."

"I had noticed that." Chris nodded. "You've been rubbing yourself against me a lot more." When Silva's cheeks turned red again, he chuckled. "Relax. It's not a big deal. In any case, we should decide what to do from here on out."

Silva calmed down and tilted her head, her cat-like eyes gaze at him with curiosity. "What should we do?"

"There are two options right now. The first is we go to the Chula Vista Catgirl Clinic and get a prescription of mating pills to help you deal with this problem. This is what most people who have a catgirl do unless she has a mate. Or we can go with the second option."

"What's the second option?" asked Silva.

Chris took a deep breath and stared directly into Silva's eyes as he answered her. "You become my catpanion."

Catpanion was the term used to describe a catgirl who was, in a sense, like a girlfriend or maybe even a wife. The difference between a girlfriend/wife and a catpanion was that a lot of red tape was necessary for a catgirl to become someone's catpanion. They would have to go to the nearest Catgirl Protection Bureau Office of Catpanion and Child Registration and register Silva as his catpanion. Chris would also be tested twice a year from now on to make sure he was fit both mentally and physically to be Silva's partner. It was a lot like becoming a breeder. The difference was that Chris would not be having sex with multiple random catgirls he didn't know.

Silva's eyes widened in shock. "You… you want me to be your catpanion?"

"I do," Chris said without hesitating. Tears welled up in Silva's eyes as her lips trembled. Chris felt a moment of panic. "Erm, but only if you want to become my catpanion. I'd never force you into this."

"I do! I want to be your catpanion!" Silva said suddenly.

"Okay." Chris smiled as a small moment of relief washed over him. He wouldn't say he was worried, since he felt fairly positive in her answer, but there was always that small niggling doubt when taking a step like this. "In that case, perhaps I should help you settle the problem you're having right now."

"The problem I'm—oh!" Silva blushed bright red again as her thighs squirmed. "Um… is that alright? I mean… after what happened earlier…"

"To be honest, this is as much for me as it is for you," Chris admitted. "Seeing you masturbating on my bed has left me a little hot and bothered. I don't think I'll be able to sleep like this if we just left this matter unsettled." He took a deep breath. "What I mean to say is that I want you, and I don't want to wait until we're registered to have you."

Silva trembled again, but her lips curved into a smile. It was a beautiful and genuine expression that caused Chris's insides to turn a little squishy.

"Then… um… will you take me now?" asked Silva.

"Only if you want me to," Chris said.

"I do," Silva spoke in a soft voice that was barely above a whisper.

"In that case…"

Chris scooted across the couch until he was directly in front of Silva. Taking her into his arms, he leaned his head down and placed a kiss on her lips.

They were smoother than he expected, soft, warm, and delicate. Her pliant lips retained a gentle elasticity that made him unable to resist his urge to nibble on them. He took her lower lip between his teeth. Silva released a soft mewling sound as she gripped the back of his shirt. Her nails were a bit sharp, but he didn't mind the feeling of her scratching his back.

He didn't know how long they kissed for, but Chris eventually pressed his tongue against Silva's mouth, which opened to admit him. He ran his tongue along her teeth. The feeling of her sharp canines caused a slight shiver to race through him. At the same time, as he filled her mouth with his tongue, his dick began swelling as blood rushed to it.

"Meow… ha… Chris…" Silva murmured as he pulled his head back. Her half-lidded eyes were seductive. However, her eyes went wide when he placed a hand against her crotch and pressed his finger into her pussy through her clothes. "Chris! Meow! What are you—?!"

"You're wet," Chris said, his breathing heavy. The feeling of her juices staining her pink pajama pants was making him even harder. "You know, I've never tasted a catgirl before. I wonder if they taste different from human women."

"T-that's not something you should be—mreow!"

Silva threw her head back and released a loud mewl as he slipped his hand past her waistband and began fingering her directly. She wasn't wearing panties right now. He traced his fingers along her labia. Her pussy was pulsing like a heartbeat was traveling through it. The glistening juices leaking from her stained his finger before he spread her lips apart and began rubbing her inner lips.

"Nya… meow… mreow! Ha! Ha! Mroeeeeewwww…"

Silva's body twitched as he inserted a single finger into her pussy. Her passage was tight. He wondered if his dick would even fit inside of her, but he dismissed the thought seconds later as he leaned down and began nibbling on her neck.

"Chris! Chris! Mrrreeeeooooowww! If you keep this up... if you keep doing this... I! I—"

It didn't take too long before Silva's entire body seemed to lock up as Chris began rubbing her clit with his thumb. Her teeth clenched, her stomach muscles tightened, her toes curled, and her legs stretched out as far as they could go. Nectar flowed from her pussy, leaking around his hand and drenching her pajamas and the couch. A few seconds after her orgasm, Silva slumped back against the couch and took several rasping breaths.

"Ha... hn... meow..."

Chris sat back and looked at Silva. Her forehead and neck were covered in a light layer of sweat. Her neck was wetter than his forehead because he'd been licking and nibbling on her. He watched the way her small chest heaved, slowly removed his hands from her pajama bottoms, and stared at the juices drenching his fingers.

He stuck a finger inside his mouth, tasting the odd tart flavor of her nectar. It was quite a bit different from the other women he'd slept with. Different, but not unpleasant. While he couldn't exactly compare her taste to anything else, he couldn't deny that he thought she tasted pretty good.

Kneeling on the floor before Silva, Chris grabbed the hem of her pajamas and slid them down her hips. Silva didn't seem all there. She didn't even respond when her pussy was exposed.

Chris took a moment to admire her engorged lips. They had opened up and glistened with her own juices. He was tempted to go down on her, eating her snatch and bringing her to another orgasm, but his cock was already painfully hard, and he didn't think he could wait any longer.

He removed his own pants and, leaving both their shirts on, he leaned over and grabbed her legs, spreading them apart as he lined up his shaft with Silva's vagina. He rubbed the head against her pussy.

"Silva?" he asked, causing her to blink. "Is it okay if I put it in?"

Silva blinked several more times, looked at his face, and then looked down at his dick. Her eyes widened for a second. Then she looked back at his face.

She nodded. "Um, please be gentle."

"Don't worry. I will."

Chris kept his hands on her thighs as he pressed the head of his dick into Silva's pussy, trying his best to watch both her face and his cock as it spread her lips apart. Silva's breathing had grown heavy and several mewls escaped her throat as he pushed himself into her tight passage. Once he had bottomed out, he stood still for a time, luxuriating in the feeling. Silva was probably the tightest person he'd ever slept with. Of course, she was also the smallest, so her pussy being so tight made sense.

"I feel so full," Silva mewled and released a soft purring noise from the back of her throat.

"Is that a good thing?"

"It is…"

"I'm about to begin moving now," Chris said.

"Yes. Do it. Please," Silva moaned and mewled.

Chris rocked his hips, sliding his dick out of her pussy and pushing it back in. He started slow and worked his speed up, until a gentle slapping sound echoed around the room as his balls hit her ass cheeks.

The sensation of her cunt sucking him in every time he thrust his hips forward and trying to keep him contained when he pulled back was an experience he'd never felt before. The gentle sucking motion engulfing his cock further stimulated him, enhancing the feeling. Her walls were warm, wet, and tight. The sensations her body caused were electric.

As he gently fucked her, Silva's expression changed. Her eyes clenched shut as she bit her lower lip. He let go of her legs and placed his hands on either side of her body, pressing them firmly against the couch so he could get more leverage. The moment he did this, her legs locked around his waist, heels digging into his lower back as she reached out with her hands and placed them around his neck, pulling him down into a kiss.

Her tongue filled his mouth, stirring up the saliva between them and making his cock swell. A powerful pressure was building up in his lower abdomen and balls as Silva kissed him with all her might and her pussy sucked him in. He was barely able to breath as they continued. Their nasally gasps, grunts, and mewls filled the atmosphere, mixing with the lewd noises as he stirred up her insides with his cock.

"C-Chris!" Silva suddenly cried. "Your cock! Your cock is—it's—Meow!! I can't hold... it's too much! I! I! MREOW!!!"

Chris grunted as Silva's pussy tightened around him so much that he couldn't even move. At the same time, his balls suddenly swelled and an intense sensation washed over him. He thrust his dick as far into her as he could, his head pressing against something near the back of her vagina. Then he released his cum inside of her. His dick twitched several times as he shot several loads into her pussy.

As he pulled his now flaccid cock out, a mixture of cum and Silva's love nectar dripped from her pussy, leaking down and dripping onto the couch. He would have to clean that, but he didn't mind. Meanwhile, Silva was breathing like she'd just run several days without rest. Her body was slumped over as she sat on the couch.

"Silva… how do you feel?" asked Chris.

"I feel… I feel… mreow…" Silva said.

Chris chuckled as he leaned over, placed a hand underneath Silva's chin, and raised her head so he could kiss her lips. Silva released a faint purring noise in the back of her throat.

"We should go to bed now," Chris said as he leaned back.

"M… kay…"

Silva tried to stand up, but the moment she did, her legs wobbled and she fell into Chris's chest. Seeing that she couldn't stand, Chris scooped her into his arms and walked into the bedroom. He pulled back the covers and set Silva on the bed, climbed in after her, and pulled the covers over them both. As he did, Silva pressed her body against his and affectionately rubbed her face against his chest as she began purring again.

Just like that, Silva fell asleep, soft whistling sounds emitting from her mouth. Chris remained awake for a little while longer. He rubbed his hand along Silva's arm, but he was tired. Closing his eyes, he took a deep breath, and slowly slipped into slumber.

chapter 9

Chris opened his eyes as light streamed through the window. He glanced around, belatedly realizing that he was in his bed instead of sleeping on the couch like he had been for the past two weeks. As he wondered about this, his mind still locked within the haze of sleep, something shifted against him.

He looked down.

The person who had shifted against him was a young catgirl with silver hair and pale skin, Silva, whom he had taken in after discovering her unconscious underneath a bridge at Memorial Park. She was nestled against his torso. Her head rested on his shoulder as her naked, lithe body pressed into him. He could feel her nipples on his skin. An electric jolt raced through his body as memories of last night washed over him.

A smiled appeared on his face as he slowly relaxed into bed. It had been awhile since he'd been in a relationship like this. In high school, he'd had several relationships, but most of them had ended after Elsa discovered them. She never did like it when he began dating someone despite the fact that they were not even a couple. The girl was like one of those annoying younger sisters who constantly sabotaged her brother's relationships.

"I wonder how I'm going to explain this to Elsa," he said at last, but then shrugged. He would cross that bridge when he got to it.

A few minutes past like this. Chris normally would have been out of bed the moment he woke up, but a glance at his clock revealed it was still early, 5:30am, and he didn't have to get up until at least 6:00am. However, even if he was luxuriating in the feel of having a cute catgirl snuggled against him, Chris had never been the type who could simply stay still.

Eventually growing bored just lying there, Chris gently rolled Silva off him, until she was lying on her back. As he did, he noticed that her shirt had been removed some time during the night and was now sitting ruffled on the bed. He was certain she'd been wearing it when they went to bed. He had only taken off her pants. Similarly, Chris was dressed in nothing but a shirt as he had removed his pants last night when they had sex.

Sitting up in bed, Chris removed his shirt and tossed it over the side. Then he shifted until he was lying on his side and looking at Silva.

The catgirl was still breathing deeply and evenly, a soft whistling sound escaping from her lips, as her chest rose and fell. He glanced at her small breasts. Chris generally preferred bigger ones, but he wouldn't deny there was something attractive about her cute chest and the way her puffy nipples stiffened as the air hit it.

A few minutes passed before he decided to wake Silva up. Leaning down, he kissed her cheek, then moved up and kissed her again. He trailed kisses along her face before eventually reaching her lips. As he pressed his mouth against hers, Silva began kissing back. She wasn't awake yet. Her eyes were still closed. But perhaps she instinctively recognized who was kissing her.

Because he hadn't gotten a chance to play with them last night, Chris took this moment to cup one of her breasts in his left hand. As he massaged her breast, her nipple quickly stiffened into a point, and he began slowly tugging on it. He pinched it between his fingers and poke it back into her chest.

"Mreeeooooowwww purr…"

A soft sound emerged from Silva's throat as he continued his ministrations. Finally, her eyelids opened, revealing two different colored eyes. When he saw this, Chris pulled back, though he continued to massage her chest.

"Good morning," he greeted her.

"Chris… Good meowning," Silva said, though her words turned into a moan when he pinched her nipple. "T-that feels really good."

"I can make you feel better, if you want."

"Y-yes please. I want—mreow!"

Silva's hands went into Chris's hair as he leaned down and took her nipple into his mouth, swirling his tongue around it before flicking up and down once. He nibbled on it as he removed his left hand from her mouth and let it travel across her stomach. Her belly twitched as he touched it. However, he soon reached the area between her thighs. Cupping her pussy with his hand, he rubbed his fingers against her labia and came away with quite a bit of love nectar.

"You're already so wet," Chris said.

"T-that's because I feel so—mreow! So good!" Silva cried out. "Chris! I don't—meow!—don't think I can take anymore! Please!"

Silva's face had scrunched up in pleasure. Her breathing was ragged and heavy as she opened her mouth. He looked down from her face to her chest. Even though her breasts were not large, they did shake a bit as her body twitched. He never thought he'd call a pair of boobs adorable, but that was the only word he could think of to describe hers.

"How can I say no to that face?" Chris said as he sat up.

Grabbing her legs, Chris held them up and spread them apart, revealing her dripping pussy, which had already become puffy with arousal. He didn't hesitate to move his dick until the tip pressed against it. Slowly inserting his cock inside of her, Chris enjoyed both the feeling and the sight as he started rocking his hips back and forth.

"H-how is it?" asked Chris.

"Good! So good! Mreow! More! I want mreow!"

Chris increased his pace, causing her small breasts to bounce as his balls gently slapped against her ass cheeks. Her legs shook as he continued to hold them. Meanwhile, Silva had gripped the bed with both hands and had thrown her head back against the pillows as she released numerous cute noises that, for whatever reason, really turned Chris on. He wanted to hear more of those lovely sounds.

"Top! Mreow! Chris! I! Haaa! Mreow! On top please!"

Her words were punctuated by pants and meowing, but Chris figured out what she wanted and rolled them over. Now on top, Silva arched her back and began grinding her hips.

There was something sensational about the feeling of her tight walls squeezing him from this position. It felt like he was reaching deeper than before. A slick wetness trickled from her pussy and caused a trail to drip down his hips.

A strong smell hung in the air. Sweat glistened along their bodies. Chris was mesmerized by the sight of Silva riding him to a climax. The way her flat stomach and small chest heaved and shook made him feel like he was ten seconds from exploding.

It didn't take a long time for him to climax. His balls suddenly tightened as pressure built up in his lower abdomen. Then all that energy was released as he came inside of her pussy, which pulsated and tightened around his cock like she was trying to milk him. Silva released a louder cry as her entire body shuddered and twitched. Her flowing juices stained his cock as he pulled out of her with a wet plop.

"Ha... ha..."

Chris watched with satisfaction as Silva's limp body heaved. The pronounced rise and fall of her chest, glistening with sweat, made him feel like he could probably go another round. However, when he looked at the clock and saw that it was 5:56am, he knew they wouldn't be able to go again.

"Want to take a shower with me?" Chris asked.

Silva blinked several times and looked at him before nodding.

Perhaps it was the result of last night or maybe this morning, but Silva needed help standing up. Her legs were wobbly. Chris allowed her to lean into him as they traveled into the bathroom.

They spent a longer time in the shower than was probably necessary. Chris and Silva took turns helping wash each other. Silva washed his body with soap, while he washed her hair, body, and tail with the new catgirl products he'd bought for her. She seemed to love the shower cap, which kept the water from getting into her eyes when he washed her hair. It looked a lot like the rim of a big round hat without the top.

After getting clean, they got dressed.

Chris wore basic jeans and a white T-shirt with a winking two-tailed, red-haired fox girl on the front. Silva had chosen to wear something more feminine. A blue dress adorned her body. The light blue color went well with her silver hair and blue/gold eyes. It had puffy sleeves and a bow tied into the back. After she was dressed, Chris tied her long hair into a fishtail style ponytail with bangs traveling down to frame either side of her face.

Unfortunately, Chris ended up spending so much time on her hair that it was nearly time for him to leave when he finished. He was only able to make a quick breakfast of scrambled eggs before he had to grab all of his stuff and rush toward the door.

"I have to go, but I'll see you when I get back!" Chris said to Silva.

"W-wait!" Silva suddenly called just as he was rushing out the door. He paused and turned back to Silva, who stood with her hands clasped in front of her, twiddling her thumbs. "I'm your catpanion now… so, um, you can't leave without giving me a kiss goodbye."

"You're right. I'm sorry." Chris gave her a sheepish smile. "I was in such a rush that I wasn't being a very good boyfriend."

Chris released the handle and walked over to Silva. Tilting her head up just a little, Chris leaned down and placed a gentle kiss on her soft lips. Silva stood on her tiptoes as she kissed him back, her hands on his chest, her tail sticking straight up into the hair. When she leaned back, her cheeks were dusted with a light shade of pink.

"Have a good day," she said.

"Thank you. You too."

Chris smiled at her one last time, and then he was shutting the door behind him and traveling out of the apartment complex.

****

Thursday was one of his shorter days. He had Quantitative Analysis at 7:35am to 11:30am, followed by Psychology from 1:15pm to 2:15pm.

Quantitative Analysis was probably his least favorite course of all. It was a class that taught a technique to understand behavior by using mathematical and statistical modeling, measurement, and research. Its aim was to represent a given reality in terms of a numerical value. It was often employed for several reasons, including measurement, performance evaluation, or valuation of a financial instrument and predicting real-world events, such as changes in a country's gross domestic production.

Chris hated math. The only reason he was taking this course was because it was required. A certified Catgirl Doctor needed to also understand finances and business management since running a clinic was also part of being a doctor. He had already taken a course in Business Management and Finances, so now he was taking this one.

Despite how much he despised everything that had to do with math, Chris took diligent notes as he listened to the teacher lecture them on how the US government relied on quantitative analysis to make monetary and other economic policy decisions. It was an incredibly boring lecture too. His teacher, an older man with gray hair and a large gut, spoke in a voice so dry he would have rather listened to static blaring from an old TV.

Sadly, this class was about four hours long.

Aside from spending his time in class listening to the teacher, Chris also thought about what he'd be doing today. He did kickboxing six days a week, so he'd be heading to the kickboxing center after classes let out, but then he wanted to see if maybe he and Silva could travel to the nearest Catgirl Protection Bureau Office and register her as his catpanion.

When class ended, Chris placed his notes in his backpack, stood up, and slung it over his shoulder before making his way outside. He wandered to The Habit Burger Grill, where he got himself a charbroiled hamburger.

As he sat down at one of the tables, drinking some water and munching on a burger as he went over his notes, someone called out to him.

"Hey, Chris. It's quite the coincidence meeting you here."

Chris looked up as a familiar blonde woman with blue eyes greeted him. She was dressed in a fashionable skirt and jacket combination, with simple earrings in her ears and a crop top underneath her jacket. Her hair had been styled into ringlets today. Whenever she moved, they would bounce like coiled springs.

"Anastasia." Chris smiled as he greeted the woman. "You have classes today too, huh?"

"Yes, but I only have one," Anastasia said.

"Lucky." Chris groaned as he set his burger down. "I just finished Quantitative Analysis, the most boring class ever, and I have another class at one. Fortunately, Psychology is just an hour long, but the teacher sounds like a drone. Her lectures have put more than a few students to sleep."

Anastasia grinned. "You mean Professor Estis, don't you? She's rather famous for being one of the most monotonous teachers in school."

"I believe it."

As they spoke, Anastasia studied him with a keen eye as she placed a hand to her chin. Chris blinked when her eyes narrowed as if she had noticed something about him.

"Is something wrong?" he asked.

"You seem different from the last time I saw you," she muttered.

"Um… you just saw me the other day," Chris pointed out. "I'm not sure what can change in a single day. You sure you're not just imagining things?"

"No, no. There is definitely something different about you today," she confirmed, nodding several times as she pursed her lips. "I can tell. I just don't know what's changed."

Chris wondered if maybe she could somehow tell that he'd had sex. He remembered his mom once saying something about the strength and perceptiveness of a woman's intuition, though he hadn't put much stock into her words at the time. On the other hand, Chris wasn't acting any differently from how he normally acted... at least, he didn't think so.

Before he could say anything, a new voice called out.

"Hey, Anna! Are you going to order something, or should I order for you while you talk to your boyfriend?"

The person who spoke was another woman, a girl with light brown hair and an olive tan, and it looked like she was part of a group. There were two other women with her. One of them was a redhead with pale skin and freckles. The other was a lean woman with dark skin and long hair done up in a perm.

"I'll be right there," Anastasia called out before turning to him. "I know you've already got your food, but do you want to eat with us?"

Chris thought about her question for a moment, but in the end, he didn't see anything wrong with eating together. He smiled and shrugged his shoulders.

"I don't see why not? Want me to save these seats for you?" he asked.

"That would be great."

Anastasia went back over to her friends as they stood in front of the counter. Chris watched them order their food, pay for it, and then make their way over to him. The other three girls were looking at him with smiles as they giggled and said something to Anastasia, who bumped one of them with her hips. It looked like they were talking about him.

"Thanks for letting us sit with you," the one with light brown hair said. "My name is Olivia. This is Tasha and Catherine." She pointed to the dark-skinned woman and the redhead respectively. "And you already know Anastasia."

"It's a pleasure to meet you three," Chris greeted them. "My name is Chris."

"We know." Tasha grinned at him. "Anastasia won't shut up about you."

Chris raised an eyebrow as he glanced at Anastasia, who quickly looked away. The woman crossed her arms and huffed at her friends.

"I've only mentioned him a few times. You are completely exaggerating." Mastering her blush, she looked back at him. "Don't listen to them. They like to make mountains out of molehills."

"Yeet. We do not," said Catherine with a giggle.

Chris didn't know what "yeet" meant.

"It's fine," he said with a wave of his hand before smiling at Anastasia's three friends. "I hope the things she's been saying about me are good."

"Depends on what you think is good." Olivia shrugged as a dazzling and mischievous smile crossed her face. "Anastasia has, on many occasions, mentioned a certain hottie in her Catgirl Biology classes."

"Oh, shut up! I do not!" Anastasia said.

Chris felt his smile become a little stiff as he listened to the three women tease their friend. He'd been around the block enough times to know what was happening here. The women were needling their friend, telling the man she thought was attractive that she was attracted to him, which was a not-very-subtle way of letting him know that Anastasia was interested in him. All this was done in an effort to make the man ask the girl out.

Had this been before he met Silva, he probably would have been interested in her. Anastasia was a great person. She was kind, helpful, and intelligent. The fact that she was training to be a Catgirl Doctor was proof enough of that. She was also a gorgeous woman. Long blonde hair, beautiful blue eyes, and a great sense of fashion. She had a body that models would kill for and men drooled over. Even with the jacket on, he could see her toned stomach thanks to her midriff revealing shirt and large breasts straining against the fabric, confined by a simple bra. Her long legs were visible beneath the short skirt, which only went halfway down her thighs.

However, he now had Silva in his life. More than that, he and Silva had sex. While there was nothing in the law that said a person couldn't have a catpanion and get married to another woman, very few women would ever be willing to marry a man who had a catpanion. Chris remembered his conversation a few weeks ago with Anastasia. She had said she would break up with someone if she found out the man she was dating lived with a catgirl.

As Chris debated whether he should pull Anastasia aside and let her know about his new relationship, his cellphone suddenly rang. The four girls stopped talking and turned to stare at him.

He smiled and stood up. "Can you please excuse me for a moment?"

"Of course." Anastasia smiled at him as she reached out and tucked a strand of hair behind her ear.

"Thanks."

Chris wandered to a quiet corner of the restaurant and accepted the call.

"Hello?" he said as he pressed the phone to his ear.

"Hello, is this Chris Redford?" asked a female voice on the other end.

"It is," he said. "May I ask who this is?"

The voice sounded familiar, but he couldn't place it.

"This is Ellen Demire with the San Diego Police Department's Catgirl Protection Bureau branch office. We met several weeks ago when you called in to report a case of catgirl abuse."

"I remember." Chris paused as he recalled the woman with pale skin and red hair and her dark-skinned partner. "If you're calling me, does that mean you've discovered something in the case and need Silva and me to come in?"

"You're perceptive. Yes, that is it exactly. We've recently come across a man who was reported for catgirl abuse who matches the description Silva gave us. His name is Markus Flint. We would like you two to come in sometime today. We want Silva to confirm his identity for us."

Chris ran a hand through his hair as he thought about what he should do. Of course he would go to the police department with Silva, but he also had a lot of things he needed to do today.

"Do you have a specific time you need me in by? I have college classes right now."

"If you can come in some time before five in the evening, that would be great."

"I understand. I'll let Silva know what's happening, and we'll come in before then."

"Thanks."

Chris hung up, pocketed his phone, and made his way back over to the four women, all of whom were staring at him with inquisitive eyes as he sat down. He met those stares with an even gaze before turning to Anastasia.

"Sorry about that. I got a call from the police."

"The police!" Olivia and Tasha shouted so loudly the other patrons sitting down to eat glanced over at them.

Anastasia looked at him oddly, but then she seemed to remember something and leaned forward. "Is it about…"

"It is." Chris nodded when she trailed off. "It seems they found someone who matches the description Silva gave them. They asked us to come in so Silva can confirm his identity."

Anastasia bit her lip, nodded, and leaned back. While the other women looked confused, she understood what Chris meant since he'd already told her about Silva's circumstances. That was probably why she also still expressed an interest in him. As far as she was aware, Silva was just someone he had temporary custody over until this matter was settled.

While Chris wanted to tell her about his and Silva's new relationship, a good opportunity never presented itself as the other three women needled him with all kinds of questions. In the end, Chris left the restaurant without having ever mentioned how Silva had become his catpanion.

****

The San Diego Police Department that Chris and Silva traveled to was on El Camino Real, which was between Del Mar Heights and Verona. They needed to take several trams to reach it, and it took them about 53 minutes. During that time, Silva had nervously clung to his arm as they sat on the various trams, her tail flicking back and forth with agitation.

The San Diego Police Department on El Camino sat on a hill, was longer than it was wide, and was built with a slit curve. It had a gated parking lot that could only be accessed by people who had the gate code. Fortunately, Chris and Silva had not driven a car to get there. Chris didn't even have a car.

When they entered, it was to find a mostly empty waiting room with several places to sit and a long counter that curved in the shape of a U. Chris glanced at the only two people aside from himself and Silva. Both of them were human. One of them was a young woman around his age. The other was a middle-aged man. They weren't sitting together, so he assumed they were here for different reasons.

He walked up to the counter, where an older man in a police uniform was sitting. The man looked up, dark eyes flashing as he looked at Chris, then Silva, and then went back to Chris.

"Name and reason for visiting?" the man inquired as he placed his hands against a keyboard.

"Chris Redford and Silva," Chris said. "We received a call from Ellen Demire a little while ago and were asked to come in and ID someone for her."

"Ah." The man suddenly seemed to understand, as he nodded once and typed something on his keyboard. "You're here because of Ellen. I'll contact her and let her know that you've arrived. She'll be out in a few minutes, so just sit tight."

"Will do."

Chris led Silva over to the chairs and sat down. As he did, Silva leaned into him, clinging to him in a way she hadn't done since they first began living together. She was shivering.

"Are you scared?" he asked.

Silva nodded. "I don't know… if I can do this. I don't want to see him again. If I could help it, I would rather forget about what happened."

"I understand." Chris placed his free hand over Silva's and gave it a reassuring squeeze. "However, you don't have to worry about him trying anything. I'm going to be right beside you the entire time. Once you've confirmed that he's the man who abused you, we can leave and you'll hopefully never have to see him again." He paused. "You'll also help prevent other catgirls from suffering the same fate by putting a criminal behind bars."

Silva nodded once more and slowly relaxed, taking a deep breath to calm herself.

The other two people inside of the waiting room watched them. While the man was wearing a disapproving frown for some reason, the woman looked at them with a smile.

Minutes after they sat down, a familiar redhead appeared from a doorway on their left. She looked around before spotting them. Her eyes brightened as she made her way over. Chris and Silva stood up and greeted the woman.

"Officer Demire," Chris said. "It's good to see you."

"You too, though I wish our circumstances were different," Officer Demire said. "If you two could please follow me, I'll lead you to where we are holding the suspect."

"We won't have to meet him, will we?" asked Chris as he and Silva followed Officer Demire through the doorway and into a long hallway filled with windows. Several doors on either side led to what he guessed were offices.

Officer Demire shook her head. "While you will have to see him to confirm his identity, he will not be able to see you. We currently have him locked inside of an interrogation room. We use a one-way mirror for interrogations. You'll simply stand in the room on the other side of the mirror and confirm whether or not this is the man who raped you. He won't even know you are here."

Silva remained stoically silent as she listened, her cheeks still a little pale, though she also looked a bit relieved that he wouldn't be able to see her. Chris was sure that had been her biggest worry. He couldn't even imagine how terrifying it would be to confront your rapist.

They were eventually led into a room that literally contained nothing except a large glass panel on one side and a person. The person was not Officer Hudson, as he expected, but a man with graying hair, a trim beard, and a fit body with just a bit of a gut hanging over his belt. When they entered, the man looked from Officer Demire, to Chris, to Silva, where it paused.

"Officer Demire, is this them?" he asked, looking back at Officer Demire.

"It is," she confirmed as she walked further into the room.

"Good. I'll leave this to you."

The officer, who Chris assumed was maybe a captain or something, nodded at them and left the room.

Officer Demire turned to them and smiled at Silva.

"This is your part. All we need from you is to look into that window and tell us whether or not the person on the other side is your abuser."

"… Okay," Silva said with a brave nod.

Chris held her hand as they walked over to the window and looked inside. On the other side of the window was a simple room with a rectangular table and two chairs. It looked like the standard interrogation rooms from crime TV shows like *CSI Miami* and *Law and Order*. Sitting in one of those chairs was a pale man with a buzzed head, an unshaven beard, and a sunken look in his angry eyes. His clothing was crumpled and creased. It looked like he had been a little roughed up during the arrest.

"That's him," Silva confirmed. "That's the man who kept me and several other catgirls locked up and abused us."

"Okay," Officer Demire took a deep breath, released it, and smiled. "That's all we need from you. Let me walk you back out."

While the process had seemed relatively painless, Chris knew that it wasn't as simple for Silva as it had been for him. He was also wondering if this was really all they needed to do.

"Is that really all you need?" he asked as they walked down the hall. "Will a simple confirmation be enough?"

"Not all cases are simple," Officer Demire admitted. "We can't persecute someone simply based on a victim's testimony. All suspects are innocent until proven guilty. However, we already have a lot of evidence against him.

Blood samples. Sperm samples. Hair samples. Etc. We also checked out his house and discovered what appears to be a prison cell in his basement. There were several catgirls locked up down there when we searched it."

Chris could only nod. With that much evidence, it would be impossible for them not to convict him. In truth, it sounded like they didn't really need Silva to confirm his identity to convict the man, but he was sure the police had wanted her confirmation just so she could know that her abuser would be placed behind bars.

"Um, Officer Demire?" Silva suddenly spoke up.

"What is it?" asked Officer Demire.

"Was there… a dark-skinned catgirl named Kuro among those who were locked up?" asked Silva.

Officer Demire opened the door that led into the waiting room and held it open for them, her face thoughtful as she searched her memory. After a moment, she shook her head.

"I don't remember any dark-skinned catgirls being present." She paused. "Is this Kuro a friend of yours?"

Silva nodded. "Big Sister Kuro was one of the other catgirls locked up with me. She was very kind and strong. She was normally kept sedated, but it wore off on the day when he tried to take me to his room a second time. She attacked him just after he opened our cage and told me to run. It was only thanks to her that I escaped."

"She sounds like an admirable woman." Officer Demire smiled. "I'll look into her whereabouts for you."

"Thank you," Silva said.

Chris and Silva left the police department after that, hopped onto a bus, and returned home almost an hour later. It was late at night by the time they arrived. They hadn't eaten dinner, so Chris whipped up a simple mahi mahi salad with kale, shredded cabbage, black beans, olives, cherry tomatoes, and avocado with a chipotle dressing made from pureed chipotle peppers.

They ate mostly in silence. Chris was watching Silva, who seemed to be thinking deeply about something. She ate slower than him, so he waited until she finished her food, then took both their plates to the dishwasher while she went over to the couch and sat down. She didn't turn on the TV like she usually did. As he sat down beside her, Silva fell over and leaned into his shoulder.

"You okay?" he asked.

"Yes." Silva sighed as snuggled closer to him. "I feel a lot better. I was nervous going into the police department, but I'm relieved to know Markus is going to be persecuted and thrown in jail."

"Me too."

"But I'm also worried about Kuro," she said.

"I understand." Chris shifted so he could place his arm around Silva and pull her close. The gentle scent of her shampoo pervaded his nose, a mixture of lavender and something sweeter like honey. He leaned down and pressed a kiss to the crown of her head. "I'm sure the police will find her. When they do, we can go visit her to see how she is doing."

"Thank you," Silva said.

"You're welcome."

"I mean it." Silva looked up at Chris, her wide heterochromatic eyes containing his image reflected in them. "You really helped me out. You took me in, fed me, and let me stay here even though you didn't have to. You could have just ignored me when you found me, but you didn't. You... you gave me a home. I can't tell you how grateful I am."

Chris smiled at Silva as he stroked her cat ears, which twitched a little. He placed her ears between his thumb and index finger, stroking the inside of her ear with his thumb, which caused Silva to stiffen as a soft purr emitted from her throat.

"You know, when I first found you and let you stay here, I was very worried about how this would all turn out. I kept thinking about what you had been through and sometimes wondered if you'd be more comfortable with a woman being your guardian." Silva's eyes turned horrified, which caused him to chuckle softly before rubbing her ears some more. "I just didn't know if you'd be okay with a man looking after you given what happened… but it all worked out. We didn't really have any problems. What's more, I've grown to really love being with you. So, if anything, you don't really need to thank me."

Silva's sniffled as her eyes teared up. She leaned forward and buried her face into his chest. In response, Chris wrapped his arms around the catgirl and pulled her close. He buried his nose in her hair and closed his eyes.

"I love you, Chris."

"I love you too."

They remained like that for several hours, just the two of them, basking in each other's presence and the feelings they shared, until they eventually fell asleep like that on the couch.

~Fin

I LOVE YOU
...

Afterward

Hello, everyone! For those who are reading one of my stories for the first time, welcome. My name is Brandon Varnell, and I am a light novel author.

Catgirl Doctor was originally meant to be a cute and fluffy story about a college student and his harem of catgirls. My plan for this series was that Chris Redford would one day be caught in the rain. He would find shelter at a pastry shop, where he would meet and fall in love with Silva—a catgirl pastry chef. If you've played the visual novel Nekopara, then you may know why I was planning to make her a pastry chef. It was supposed to be my nod to the series that inspired this one. The MC in Nekopara is a pastry chef who runs his own confectionery and works with his harem of catgirls.

That's right. This series was inspired by Nekopara.

I know. You are shocked.

I'm not sure what happened that turned my series into something so dark. I think part of it might be my cynical nature. Maybe I just have trouble believing humans can live in harmony with a species like catgirls. I think if catgirls really did exist, there would be people like Markus Flint, who would be more than willing to enslave and abuse them.

Another part of why this series turned so dark might also be due to social media. I wrote this story around the time the MeToo movement became really big in the anime dubbing industry. Since I check my social media at least several times a day, I couldn't go 24 hours without seeing at least 10-15 sexual abuse/harrassment posts.

I am not going to get into politics in this afterword. If you know anything about me, then it is that I hate discussing politics. I'm sure everyone has their opinions on these subjects. I know I have my own opinions. However, you are here to read an entertaining story, not read my blathering rants about politics and social justice, and I am here to write what you will hopefully find to be an entertaining story.

Thoughts on politics and social justice aside, while I might be cynical, I do have hopes and ideals for humanity. I hope that for every Markus Flint, there are at least one-hundred Chris Redfords. That for every person who would abuse a catgirl or their fellow human, there are at least a thousand who would step in to defend the abused.

You'll notice that I have not introduced the catgirl harem in this volume. I was going to, but then I reconsidered introducing the other two catgirls in volume 1. My reasons are, of course, because of the sensitive content this volume deals with. Rape is a serious issue. I don't think adding a harem into a volume that so heavily deals with this subject was appropriate.

I plan on introducing the other two members of Chris' harem in the next volume.

Before I end this afterword, I would like to give thanks to several people.

I would like to thank my artist for this series. Liremi is a new artist I hired for Catgirl Doctor. She does a glorious job. I think her artwork is super adorable and the erotic scenes are sexy as fuck.

To my editor, thank you for fixing the syntax and writing in this manuscript. The story flows a lot more smoothly now.

To my proofreaders, thank you for correcting my grammar mistakes, misspellings, and homonym errors. Nothing is more embarrassing than when you use to, too, and two incorrectly in your writing.

And finally, to you readers, thank you very much for reading this story. I really do hope you enjoyed it. Also, to the new readers, I am very sorry you guys jumped headlong into such a dark story. I hope you weren't put out by it and will stick around for the next volume.

~Brandon Varnell

Like manga? Brandon is adapting his American Kitsune light novel series into a manga on Patreon!

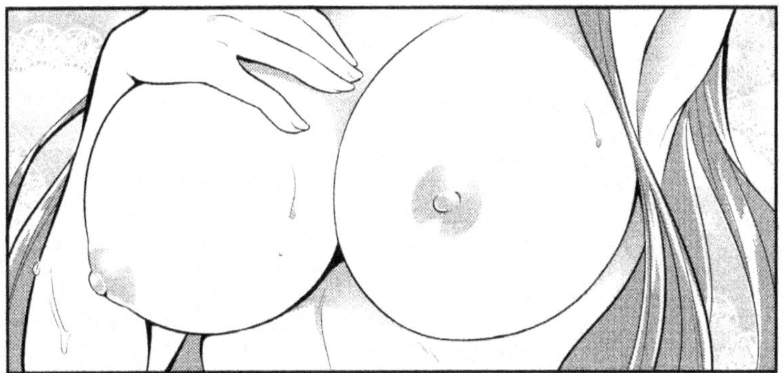

HAVE YOU EVER EXPERIENCED ONE OF THOSE LIFE-CHANGING INSTANCES? AN EVENT SO MOMENTOUS THAT, YEARS LATER, YOU'RE STILL MARVELING AT HOW IT CHANGED YOUR LIFE?

I HAD ONE OF THOSE. IT HAPPENED A WHILE AGO

EVEN TO THIS DAY, THROUGH ALL THE CHANGES THAT HAVE HAPPENED, THROUGH ALL THE EXPERIENCES THAT I'VE BEEN THROUGH, I STILL CAN'T BELIEVE HOW THIS ONE MOMENT CHANGED MY LIFE FOREVER.

NO MATTER WHAT CAME AFTER, OUR FIRST MEETING IS SOMETHING THAT I'LL ALWAYS REMEMBER.

ESPECIALLY SINCE, AT THE BEGINNING OF THIS TALE, I THOUGHT SHE WAS NOTHING BUT AN ORDINARY FOX WITH, UNORDINARILY ENOUGH, TWO BUSHY RED TAILS.

LIFE

.

.

.

.

.

.

.

.

.

IT HITS YOU WHEN YOU LEAST EXPECT IT TO.

Hey, did you know?
Brandon Varnell has started a Patreon
You can get all kinds of awesome exclusives
Like:

1. The chance to read his stories before anyone else!
2. Free ebooks!
3. exclusive SFW and NSFW artwork!
4. Signed paperback copies!
5. His undying love!
Er... maybe we don't want that last one, but the rest is pretty cool, right?

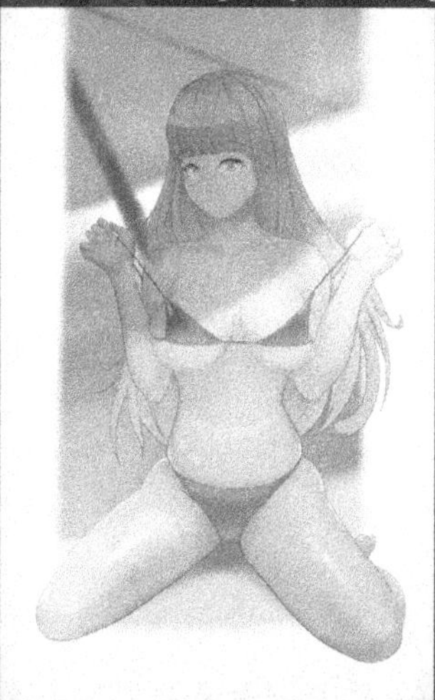

To get this awesome exlusive conent go to:
https://www.patreon.com/BrandonVarnell
and sigh up today!

American Kitsune
volumes 1-12
are available now!

Volumes 1-6
are available now!
A
Most
Unlikely
Hero

Volumes 1-2
available on Amazon and Kindle
WIEDERGEBURT
LEGEND OF THE REINCARNATED WARRIOR

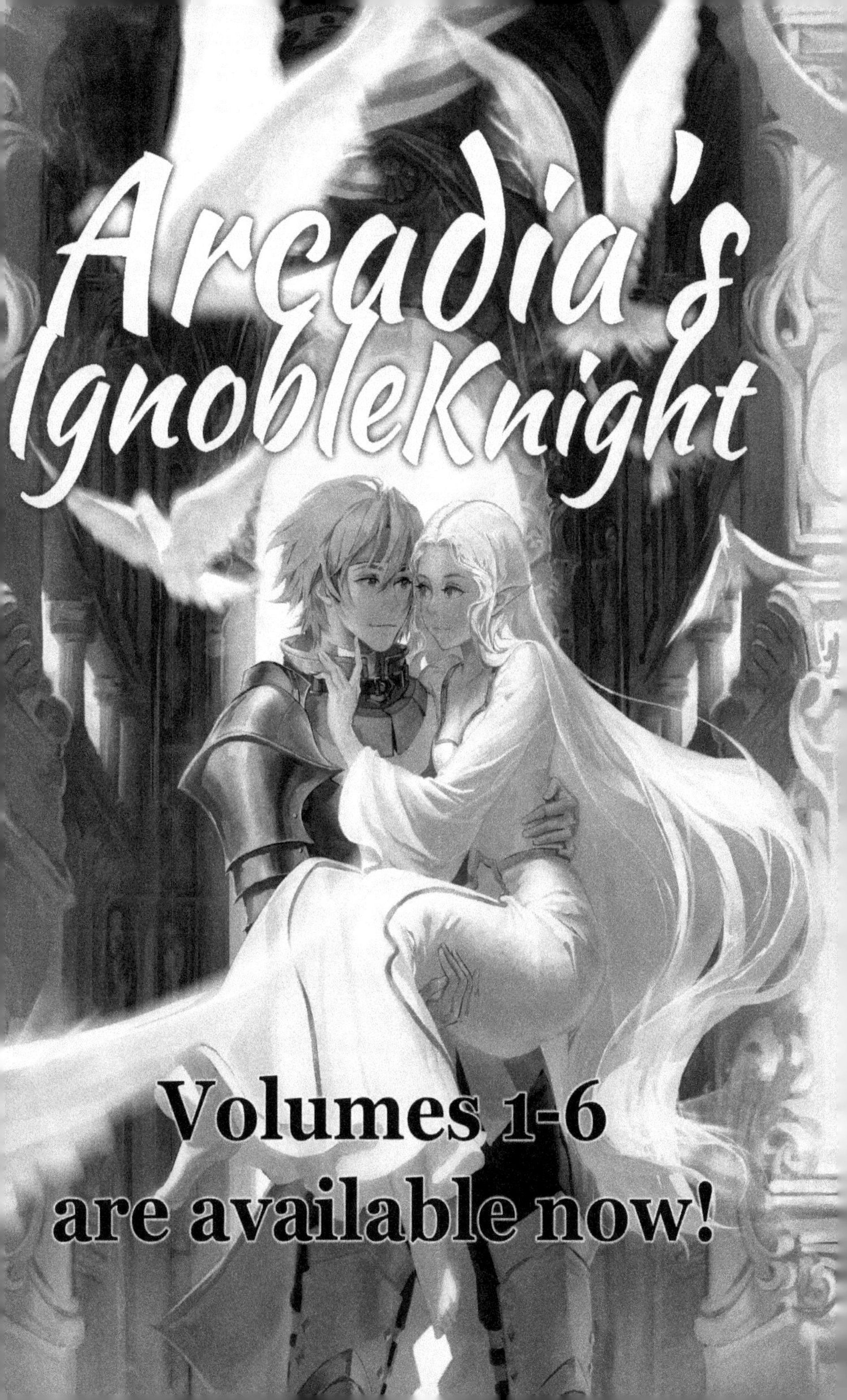
Arcadia's IgnobleKnight
Volumes 1-6
are available now!

The Complete Series is available now on paperback and Amazon Kindle!

JOURNEY of a BETRAYED HERO

Volumes 1 & 2 are available on
paperback,
Amazon,
and Kindle Unlimited
Swordsman
Of the
Rift 2

The Executioner Series
The complete series
is available now!